BEYOND
THE VERDE RIVER

BEYOND THE VERDE RIVER

•

S.J. Stewart

AVALON BOOKS
NEW YORK

Ste

PRINTED IN THE UNITED STATES OF AMERICA
ON ACID-FREE PAPER
BY HADDON CRAFTSMEN, BLOOMSBURG, PENNSYLVANIA

To my grandsons:

Dusty
Christopher
Jason
and
Trevor

And to my step-grandsons:

Donny
and
Caleb

Chapter One

The saloon was crowded and noisy but Jake Lockridge kept his mind on business, which was the poker game he was sitting in on. Although he was thirsty, he declined to drink, for a man needed to have his wits about him in a card game. Besides, he couldn't afford the morning-after hangover.

He shifted his weight in the chair as the gray-haired man to his left began to deal. Jake figured on it being his last hand since his luck had alternated between tepid and bad all evening, and he'd lost all the money he cared to lose. But to his surprise, when he picked up his cards he saw they had possibilities. He tossed away a seven, keeping two kings and a pair of tens.

"One," he said to the dealer, and picked up the card that was slid to him.

When he saw it was the king of clubs, it was only

1

through self-discipline that he was able to maintain a poker face. The others had drawn two cards apiece and his chances looked good. Taking care not to scare his opponents into tossing in their hands, he played the full house for all he was worth. When the hand was over, Jake dragged in enough to make up for his losses plus a few dollars extra.

He didn't figure his skimpy winnings would be enough to cause hard feelings when he cashed in, but he was dead wrong. The rank-smelling *hombre* sitting across the table didn't like it a bit. He tossed the stub of his cigar into a nearby spittoon and gave Jake a look that would roast a scorpion.

"I guess it's about time that you learned a few things, greenhorn," he said. "Around here, you don't grab the money and run. Ante up and deal."

Jake noticed that, all of a sudden, the room got real quiet, and everyone in the vicinity of his table started backing off. His gut muscles tightened. The timing couldn't have been worse. Everyone at the table was wearing a sidearm, except for the gray-haired man who was dressed in the manner of a professional gambler, and Jake would have bet his scant winnings that the gambler was armed with a hide-out gun.

The weathered cowpoke to his right spoke up. "Aw, Nettles, let him go. He ain't won enough to buy us all a round of drinks."

"Shut up!" said Nettles. "I didn't ask for you to butt in."

His face was a mask of anger. For some reason, he

wanted to start trouble and Jake was prepared to give it to him. He looked the man called Nettles square in the eye.

"Mister, I'm through playing for the night. Now, if you want to argue about it, you can have at it."

It was clear that this wasn't the reaction the troublemaker had expected. The look of anger was replaced by one of uncertainty. Through it all, the gambler had been watching, saying nothing. Now he cleared his throat as if he were about to deal himself in.

"Look here, Nettles, we don't want any trouble, and a dead body tends to spoil the evening for everyone. Besides, the body might turn out to be your own. Ross, here, is right; this young fellow hasn't won enough to be concerned about."

Nettles was outvoted, and he didn't like it. He sat glaring at Jake, although he took care to keep both hands on the table. While everyone in the saloon watched anxiously, Jake hauled his lanky frame from the chair and cashed in his chips. Then, while keeping an eye on Nettles, he left the Oasis.

Outside on the boardwalk, he filled his lungs with fresh, cool air. A light desert wind ruffled a nearby yucca, and overhead the sky was sprinkled with stars. He figured that his Uncle Nate had been asleep for hours over at the hotel. They were leaving Arizona City at dawn, and he was in bad need of some sleep himself. So he headed in that direction, taking care to see that he wasn't being followed by the sorehead from the poker game. The brief walk felt good after all those hours of riding a chair in the hot, smoky saloon.

Due to the late hour, the lobby was dark and deserted. On his way across the room, Jake tripped over a chair and uttered a curse. After righting the offending piece of furniture, he groped his way to the staircase and made his way to the top, step by step. He was halfway down the hall when he heard a muffled footfall behind him. His hand slid to his revolver as he turned, but he was too late. A bolt of pain shot through his skull and he slid to the floor.

When he opened his eyes again, he felt the rough plank floor of the upstairs hallway beneath him. It took him a moment to remember where he was, and he had no idea how much time had passed since the attack, although it was still dark. What he did know was that his head ached, and there was a large knot at the place of impact.

He thought of the poker game, and how Nettles had insisted on keeping him at the saloon. In light of the pistol whipping, that could mean only one thing. Somebody wanted to get to Nate without interference. He pulled himself up and staggered to their room at the end of the hall. With a sense of dread at what he would find, he shoved the door open. Immediately, he knew something was wrong. Nate was a man who could out-snore a buffalo, and the room was silent. He groped his way to the table that held a coal oil lamp and fished a match from his jacket pocket. With clumsy fingers he got the mantle off and the wick lighted. In the soft lamp-glow, he saw Nate lying in a pool of his own blood. He'd been knifed without a chance to fight back.

"Nate," he whispered as he knelt beside him, cradling his uncle's head in his arms.

But it was useless. His killer must have been the attacker in the hall. Quickly, he searched Nate's pockets for the gold pieces he'd been carrying, and he wasn't surprised to find they were gone.

"Don't worry," he said to the man who'd been his friend as well as his uncle. "Whoever did this to you is going to pay for it."

Grief and guilt mixed together as Jake realized his part in Nate's death. Had he stayed at the hotel instead of spending the evening playing poker at the Oasis, his uncle would still be alive. There wasn't a doubt in his mind about Nettles being in cahoots with the killer, and he wanted to have a talk with that sidewinder in the worst way.

He left the body where it was and went back down the hall of the ghostly silent hotel. Carefully, he descended the stairs by feel, all the while listening for warning sounds. But the killer was gone.

He didn't waste any time getting back to the Oasis, where light spilled onto the street from beneath the doors. In spite of the hour, the place was still busy. Nettles, though, was gone. So were the other two poker players who'd shared his table earlier. He made his way past a couple of tables to the bar. There, over a tune from a tinny-sounding piano, the bored-looking bartender assured him that he didn't know anything of Nettles' whereabouts.

Jake left to check the other saloons, of which there were two. It turned out to be a waste of time. He figured that Nettles and the killer must be laying low by now.

Jake walked on down to the jail and rousted the town marshal from his slumber, for the marshal kept a cot at his place of business. He was a man past his prime, and one who didn't like having his sleep interrupted. But after a couple of swear words and a measure of grumbling, Marshal Jonas Rust pulled on his boots and accompanied Jake to the hotel. Jake had warned him to bring a lantern.

"Can't that tightwad Briggs keep a lamp going in this place, or at least a candle?" the marshal complained when they entered the lobby of the hotel.

Jake shared his sentiment.

Holding the lantern high, the marshal led the way to Nate's room. Inside, the lamp that Jake had lit earlier was still burning, and it was clear to see what the killer had done.

"I'm real sorry about this," the marshal said. "Was anything stolen?"

"Some gold pieces that he was carrying."

The marshal walked over to the window that looked out on the street. Dawn was breaking in the east.

"Have you got any idea as to who might have done this?" he asked.

"As a matter of fact, I can name one of the killers. At least he was in on it. Earlier this evening, I was playing cards with an *hombre* named Nettles. He was awfully anxious to keep me at the saloon, and he actually threatened me when I started to leave. Now, I know why. His partner was up here robbing and killing my uncle."

Rust frowned at the mention of Nettles' name.

"I've seen him around town, and he's a bad one. Don't know who his partner is, though, but I'll make it a point to ask."

"Don't suppose you plan on making an arrest?"

"Can't do that without witnesses or evidence and you, yourself, said that Nettles was playing cards with you when your uncle was murdered."

Jake couldn't argue his point.

"I guess there's nothing to do, except get Archie Pickard up here," the marshal went on. "He serves as the undertaker."

Jake agreed. He was thankful that he'd taken the time to bury his gold outside of town. What he'd been playing poker with were his wages as a ranch hand.

The marshal paused at the door.

"I don't suppose any of the other guests heard anything?"

"All the doors were shut tight. I couldn't even swear there are any other guests."

"Well, I'll check the register and talk to anyone who might be able to tell us anything."

"I'd like to be with you when you do."

The hotel manager, Briggs, had returned to start his day's work. In spite of his protests, the marshal read the names on his register and began knocking on doors. The only other guests included an elderly man who was partially deaf, and two women who were traveling with a baby. None of them had heard anything that would help.

"Too bad," said the marshal. "But you can rest assured, I'll keep looking for this Nettles fellow."

Jake figured he'd gotten all the help he was going to get from the local law. He went back to Nate's room and snuffed the lamp. The undertaker had already been there and taken the remains away to his establishment. Jake closed the door and went to see that Nate was properly buried. A couple of hours later, he stood beside the grave while the local parson read a passage from the Book. He was the only mourner. Instead of being soothed, though, anger welled up inside him like bitter bile. After the final "amen", he handed the parson a gold piece and walked away from the grave.

He climbed into the saddle of the dun with an odd sense that part of his life had ended. There was nothing left for him but a new beginning. But whatever the future held, he was facing it alone. He'd already dug up his little stash of gold from its hiding place and was ready to leave. With Nate's mount and two pack mules on lead ropes, he headed in the direction of a distant mountain range. His instincts were good, and he had a feeling he was being watched. His old Spencer Carbine rested in its scabbard, and a Colt .45

was strapped at his side. He also had Nate's rifle and sidearm, along with plenty of ammunition. Whatever came, he was ready for it.

He knew that Nate had tried to be careful when he'd brought with him a small part of the vast treasure he'd discovered. His uncle had kept to himself as much as possible. But towns have eyes and ears that see and hear everything. It appeared that Arizona City also had a nose for gold.

Nettles and his partner must have found out about the stash that Nate was carrying. They would also suspect that there was more, and would stop at nothing to find the source. He knew, for sure, that Nate would never have told them the location. Another sure thing was an outlaw's greed. Their greed would bring them after him. He was counting on it, for at some time and place he intended to make them pay for what they'd done.

Chapter Two

The Gila River wound its way down through the desert from the northeast. Jake kept it in sight and followed its general direction. Because he'd gotten a late start, the sun was high in the sky, and already it was bearing down unmercifully. The heat was like a blast furnace. The hot, dry wind didn't help either, for it sucked all the moisture from his pores. Overhead, a few wispy clouds interrupted the blue of the sky, but they promised no rain. Soon Jake began looking for shade.

He headed the dun closer to the river, where a line of ironwood trees was growing.

"Whoa, boy," he said. "This looks like a good place to stop until evening."

First, he picketed the animals so they could graze on what little was available. From now on, it would be his custom to stop during the hottest part of the day and travel during the cooler hours of evening and throughout the night. His instincts told him that he was still being followed, although the outlaws were taking care to stay hidden. He figured that gold was enough incentive to make Nettles and his partner track him to purgatory, if need be. What they couldn't know was that the gold he carried scarcely equaled what Nate had sent his sister, Maggie. What's more, all the gold that Nate had taken out of those far-away mountains was nothing to the amount he'd left behind, and now that he and his uncle couldn't go back and retrieve it together, Jake was going alone.

Nate had summoned him from California and told him the entire incredible story about the treasure. He'd believed that those who'd hidden it in a narrow cave, high above the desert, no longer had need of it. It was plain that the gold had set there for many years. Some of it had been coined, but most was molded into gold bars. There were dangers involved, of course, and Nate had made them clear.

"My boy, you're the only one I can trust," he'd said. "You've got good instincts, you keep your head when there's trouble, and you know how to use a gun. I'll split what we take out right down the middle, and I'll see to it that your Aunt Maggie is taken care of for the rest of her life."

Jake had accepted his offer.

Using the ironwood trees for a screen, he spread out a blanket. Before retiring, he scanned the horizon. The outlaws were nowhere in sight. He had no doubt they were out there, somewhere, but it was easy for them to hide.

He stretched out on the blanket with the carbine at hand. It was his custom to sleep lightly, and he trusted the mules to warn him if strangers approached. Then, for the first time in many hours, he slept.

At dusk, he awoke and ate a hurried meal. By the time he was ready to move on, it was dark. As soon as the sun goes down, a cooling process begins on the desert, so Jake was able to travel in relative comfort.

The solitude of the arid wilderness enveloped him, and he figured it was a good thing that he was fond of his own company. At twenty-two, he believed he was at the peak of his strength and ability. Ranch work had toughened him over the past few years. He'd worked on a spread north of the town of Los Angeles, and before that, he'd worked on his pa's farm in Ohio.

His life had changed after his pa's death, when Nate had urged him to go with him by ship to California. It had taken everything to pay for the journey, but Jake had never regretted his decision. Once they'd arrived on the pleasant California coast, though, Nate had started itching to move on to the Arizona Territory.

"It's still a rough place, but think of the opportunity, son," he'd said, trying to persuade Jake to pull up stakes again.

But none of his arguments had any effect. Jake remained behind to work on the ranch, while Nate went on alone. He heard nothing more from his uncle, until he was summoned to Arizona City on the Colorado River.

As Jake rode through the night, he watched the Big Dipper rotate around the North Star. Often, he paused to listen. This was Apache country, and a man couldn't be too careful. Occasionally, he would hear a nocturnal animal scurrying through the brush, and he enjoyed the sound of the wind as it sang through the creosote bushes. There was something wild and wonderful about the Sonoran Desert. He was beginning to understand why Nate had been so taken with it.

"It's a beautiful place." Nate had told him when he first arrived. "There's no question about it. But it's a land of extremes, and it can be deadly in a whole lot of ways. Never let your guard down, Jacob."

Jake intended to heed his advice.

Day after day, he followed the Gila River eastward toward his destination. Alone in the desert, time tended to lose its meaning. He spent the hottest hours of each day sheltered beneath a tree, or ledge, or whatever he could find. Throughout the cool nights, he rode. He would switch off between the dun and Nate's appaloosa, always keeping one of the horses fresh.

He was traveling through the land of the saguaro, the huge cactuses that appeared to stretch fat arms toward the sky. In the night, their shadowy forms looked to him like giant ghosts that had been sent to haunt the desert. Once, close to dusk, he spotted a dust devil, one of those desert whirlwinds. He recalled an old tale about how dust devils were really mischievous spirits. The way it skipped around in a wild circle-dance, picking up dirt and plant debris, it was easy to imagine that such a thing was true.

At last, he'd safely made his way through the Painted Rock Mountains and the Gila Bend Range. The men who were following him were doing so at a distance, and they were taking care to remain hidden. He'd spotted them only once, two days earlier. But they'd quickly disappeared, leaving him to wonder if he'd actually seen them at all.

Riding day after lonely day was starting to take its toll. Jake had long since tired of his own company when he happened onto a ranch. It was an isolated adobe structure, with a few desert marigolds planted near the doorway. The flowers were a sure sign that a woman lived there.

When he rode up, a man came out to greet him. He was wearing a sidearm and his face wore a wary expression. As soon as the man had stepped through the doorway, he moved to the side, leaving whoever was in the house a clear shot at Jake.

"Howdy," Jake said, understanding their need for caution. "I was just passing through and wanted to water my horses and mules."

The man sported a dark handlebar mustache and a battered hat perched precariously on his head. Jake noticed that his hand was never far from the revolver that was holstered on his hip.

"If that's all you're wantin', Mister, then you're welcome."

"Much obliged."

Jake led the animals around to the trough that was pointed out to him. The rancher, still wary, followed.

"Name's Sherwood," he said. "And you're welcome to come in for a bite when you're finished. My woman would be pleased to have company since we don't see too many folks out this way."

"Name's Lockridge, and I'd be obliged," he replied. "I kind of like to hear the sound of another human voice once in awhile, myself."

Inside the little house, he met the woman who'd held the rifle on him. Mrs. Sherwood was plump and smiling. The surfaces in her home were mostly dust-free, and in the Sonoran Desert, that meant she was a good housekeeper. A lot of women would have surrendered to the wind and sand.

"We're so glad to have you, Mr. Lockridge," she said after her husband introduced them.

Her welcome sounded genuine, and she seemed pleased to have the feet of a homely, saddle-sore cowpoke under her table. Jake was happy to discover that the woman was a good cook, as well as a good housekeeper. He showed his appreciation of her skills by digging into a sizeable bowl of rabbit stew, and helping himself to a big slab of freshly baked light-bread. This was topped off by a piece of dried apple pie. It had been a long time since he'd had such a fine meal.

"I like to see a man with a hearty appetite," said

Mrs. Sherwood as she looked on. "It makes cooking worthwhile."

"You set a fine table, Ma'am, and I appreciate the hospitality."

"You were coming from the west," Sherwood observed. "Did you see any sign of Apaches along the way?"

"No, but I was careful and traveled mostly at night. However, there is something that I need to warn you about. A couple of outlaws are following me. They're killers."

Both the Sherwoods looked alarmed, and he felt sorry to be bringing trouble to them.

"Look, it's me they're after," he assured them. "They won't want to linger. Just keep your shotgun handy and you should be okay."

"We'll be watchful," Sherwood said. "You be careful, too, young fellow."

That's what Jake intended to do. He thanked them for their hospitality. Then he climbed into the saddle and headed out. On the way, he noticed a couple of their hands bringing in some horses. He was relieved to know that the Sherwoods wouldn't be alone. Folks like them were either brave or foolish for living out here, depending on how you looked at it.

Beyond the ranch, he came to the town that Nate had told him about. It had been built on an old Hohokam settlement, and the people who lived there were calling it Phoenix. Nate had explained how the nearby Hohokam irrigation ditches had been cleaned out and were being used again. Phoenix was, indeed, like the mythical bird it had been named for.

As soon as he arrived, Jake got himself a shave and a bath. Then he rented himself a room where he slept for a few hours in an honest-to-goodness bed. When he got up, he went and replenished his supplies and bought himself another good meal. Then he mounted up, took the spare horse and the two mules, and left Phoenix behind.

He was starting the last leg of his journey to the Mazatzal Mountains. When he caught sight of them in the light of dawn, though, he had mixed feelings. A treasure was hidden up there, of course, but it was also reported to be the stronghold of both the Yavapais and the Tonto Apaches. Right now, he was thinking that Nate must have been crazy to ride into those mountains. When he started out, he hadn't even known about the gold. He'd gone on a bet, and not a very large one, at that. But that was the way Nate Lockridge did things.

Jake started looking for a place to make camp. But when he found it, somebody else was there already. The man was sprawled, face down, on the ground. Oddly, there wasn't any sign of a horse, or even that one had been there. The only tracks leading up to the man were those made by his own boots. No doubt about it, the fellow was in a bad way. Jake dismounted and went over to see if he was still alive. He poked him in the side with the toe of his boot, and was rewarded with a moan. Jake rolled him over on his back.

To his surprise it was a kid. He must have been four or five years younger than Jake.

"Help me," the kid pleaded in a voice so faint it could scarcely be heard.

Jake fetched his canteen and spilled a few drops of water onto his parched and swollen lips. The kid managed to swallow.

He grabbed for the canteen, but Jake pulled it away before he could reach it.

"More, please," he pleaded.

"Look, you've got to be sensible about this. Only take a few sips at first. Let your body get used to having water again."

He nodded like he'd understood, so Jake let him drink a little more. Afterward, the kid struggled to sit up. It was then that Jake noticed his hands lacked calluses. They were as smooth and unmarked by toil as a young girl's might be. He also noticed that if you overlooked the sunburn, the fellow had the pleasing, well-proportioned kind of face that appealed to ladies. It was a far cry from his own angular mug that had no handsomeness about it at all. Jake figured that when he wore a beard it did everyone a favor by covering a lot of homeliness.

Another thing he noticed about the stranger was his clothes. They were almost new, and they looked expensive. That is, except for the old down-at-the-heel boots he was wearing. There was something odd about the contrast.

"Thanks for saving my life," he said. "My name's Ryan Decker."

Jake told him his own name, and then asked how he got there.

"Outlaws robbed me. They took my horse, my pack mule, and all of my belongings. One of 'em even stole my new boots and left me with these stinking, worn-out pieces of leather."

He pointed to his feet, and Jake had to agree that the boot trade was mighty uneven. But at least they hadn't left him to walk barefoot over the rough, scorching terrain. The soles of his feet would have blistered up fast. It couldn't have mattered to the outlaws, though, for leaving him out in the desert without a horse or water was the same as killing him. It was just a little slower than a bullet, that was all. Jake knew that if he hadn't come by when he did, it would only have been a short time before death would have claimed Ryan Decker.

"Sounds like you had some prospecting in mind," said Jake, although Decker appeared to be too much of a greenhorn to be wandering around the Sonoran by himself.

"That was my intention," he said ruefully. "I had a map to a gold mine, and all I had to do was ride straight up to a fortune."

Jake scratched his chin where stubble was forming again.

"A gold mine?"

"Yeah. Now, I guess those owlhoots will be the ones to find it."

Jake had heard about those maps to gold and silver mines. You could buy one, plus a real good story, for a bottle of redeye back in Arizona City. While the stories were good, the maps were worthless. He imagined the outlaws were savvy enough to know it.

He left Decker to his recovery while he took care of the animals, letting them graze on the sparse vegetation. When he'd finished his chore, it was plain cussedness that made him bedevil the kid a little.

"Tell me something," he said. "If that treasure map was so all-fired valuable, how is it that you were able to get hold of it?"

He looked startled, like he'd never really thought about it before.

"I was just lucky, I guess. Up in Prescott, I ran into an old prospector who was too crippled up to travel any more. Since he couldn't use the map himself, he was willing to let me have a go at it."

Jake slapped his thigh and laughed. He had no doubt that a con-man had suckered the greenhorn into buying a worthless piece of paper that he'd probably sketched some lines on the night before.

"What's so funny?" Decker demanded to know.

"So, an old prospector traded away a rich gold mine for a bottle of whiskey."

Sarcasm crept into his voice and Decker picked up on it.

"Of course that's not what happened. I paid the old man twenty dollars for it."

Jake laughed again. The poor dumb kid didn't even realize that he'd been cheated.

"You still haven't told me what's so funny," Decker said. Jake could tell he was getting mad.

"Oh nothing. I guess twenty dollars was the top price the old man could get for the road map to riches."

This started Decker to thinking, and it was plain that he didn't like it much.

"That old man made a fool out of me, didn't he?"

Jake looked at the ground without saying anything. He figured enough was enough.

"Oh well," said Decker. "I guess that it doesn't matter, anyway, since Culebra has it now."

Jake was startled by the name. It meant "snake" in Spanish, and it was an apt description of one of the most notorious outlaws in the Territory. Jake didn't like the idea that Culebra was anywhere near.

"How many men did he have with him?" he demanded to know.

"Only three, but they were tough and well-armed. They're armed even better, now that they have my rifle and my revolver."

"Which way did they go after they left you?"

"That way," Decker said, pointing to the southwest. "I heard 'em say they were meeting up with more of their gang somewhere the other side of Phoenix. They even mentioned a couple of names: Nettles and McQuay."

Jake was startled once again. Unwittingly, Decker had told him who Nate's killers were hooked up with. Not only that, he now had the name of Nettles' partner.

He knew that Culebra was one tough *hombre*. Nobody seemed to know what his real moniker was, but Jake had seen his picture on a wanted dodger in the marshal's office.

Decker managed to get to his feet. Once there, he managed to stay on them.

"Mr. Lockridge, it looks like you've got a lot on your mind, but I've got to ask you for the loan of a horse. It's real important that I get back to civilization as soon as possible. My Grandfather Kemp is one of Prescott's leading citizens, and he'll see to it that you're amply rewarded."

Jake was surprised at his gall, or maybe it was just stupidity.

"First of all, you can drop the 'mister'," he said. "After that, you can forget about riding out of here on one of my horses. For a fact, I don't believe you could find 'civilization' with a military escort."

Decker seemed uncertain about what to do next. It turned out that he did nothing.

"Are you going to leave me here to die?" he asked.

"No, even though you've done a fool thing coming out here and getting yourself robbed and abandoned. But I'm not an outlaw. I'll make a deal with you. If you don't give me any trouble, I'll let you ride along with me on my spare horse. But remember, if you get a sudden notion to head that horse in the wrong direction, I'll shoot you."

The threat made an impression for Decker got a sober look on his face, and it was like he was seeing Jake for the first time.

Jake turned away then to get his bedroll from the dun. It was a big mistake for the next thing he knew, Decker was on his back, punching away. Luckily, the kid had gotten his fighting lessons in grammar school. Jake twisted to the right and managed to fling his assailant to the ground. But Decker rolled and sprang to his feet, a considerable accomplishment for someone who'd been near death a short time before. Decker threw a wild punch, but Jake saw it coming and ducked. Then he stepped in and hit Decker hard in the gut. There was a "whoosh" of expelled air as the greenhorn doubled over in pain.

"Had enough?" Jake inquired as he stood back, waiting.

Decker hugged himself and desperately tried to fill his lungs. It looked like all the fire had gone out of him, not that there had been much fire to begin with. He'd simply wanted to steal a horse so he could ride off, get lost, and die of thirst in the desert. No question about it, the kid was spoiled and selfish, and it made Jake mad to be attacked that way. Decker's gratitude had been short-lived.

As soon as he was breathing steady again, Jake explained the situation to him in a forthright manner: "That fellow named McQuay, the one that Culebra is going to meet, is the one who killed my uncle back in Arizona City. Nettles, his partner, was in on the killing too. Both of 'em were on my trail for days. As soon as they meet up with the rest of the gang, you can bet your last biscuit that the whole gang will be after us. And that's not to mention that this is Apache country. If any of the Yavapais or Tontos catch us, we're sure to be guests of honor at one of their more painful pastimes."

While Decker was far too reddened by the sun to turn pale, he had a look of fear in his eyes that told Jake his message had gotten through.

He went on, "The way I see it, you've got one chance to live. That's if you tag along with me and do exactly as I say. Left on your own, you're a dead man."

There was a pause while Decker mulled it over.

"Looks like I've got no choice," he said at last.

"Then remember, any more antics like this last one and you're on your own—on foot."

They were in a draw with only some scrub for shade, but they were hidden from enemy eyes, both outlaws' and Apaches'. Jake took blankets from a bedroll and tossed one to Decker. Then he spread the other in the shade of a creosote bush and stretched out on it. He'd learned to sleep lightly during his years on the ranch, and any little sound would awaken him. This was a good thing for a man with a lot of enemies.

Besides, he didn't trust Decker any further than he could lift up and throw one of those mountains.

With his rifle beside him, Jake dozed throughout the heat of the day. At dusk, they ate lightly before loading up the mules and saddling the horses. As soon as it was dark, they moved out of the draw. For a long time, they rode in silence.

"You know, Lockridge," Decker said at last, "I've been wondering why those outlaws followed you all this way. It's many a mile from here to Arizona City, so they must have had a real good reason."

Jake debated whether or not to tell him, but he guessed that Decker would figure it out sooner or later anyway.

"I know the location of some gold. Those outlaws are aware of that, or at least they suspect it. It seems that gold is a strong incentive for travel."

He was surprised to hear Decker chuckle.

"What's so funny?"

"It turns out that I'm not the only one around here who buys treasure maps."

It took a lot of effort on his part, but Jake managed to bite back a sharp remark. Decker was the kind who had a talent for rubbing people the wrong way.

"Although it's none of your business, I didn't buy some fool treasure map. My uncle got lost in the mountains, and while he was looking for shelter, he found a cache of gold."

Decker let out a low whistle.

"You're not kidding me, are you?"

"I expect you're going to find out soon enough whether I'm kidding or not."

"So that's why that outlaw killed your uncle."

"Yes, to rob him of the gold that he carried and to find out where there was a lot more like it. Fortunately, we'd buried most of it and they never found it."

"You don't think he told them the location of that cache in the mountains, do you?"

There was a tightening in Jake's chest as he thought about Nate and the killer.

"I'm certain he didn't tell them. He wouldn't have done so even to save his life, not that telling them would have saved it. McQuay would have killed him anyway."

"Where were you when it happened?"

Decker's question hurt, but he decided to answer it. After all, it was only fair that he owned up to his own stupidity.

"As it happens," he confessed, "I was in a saloon down the street from the hotel, playing cards with Nettles and two other fellows. Nettles tried to keep me there, and it wasn't hard to do until I took a notion to leave. But by the time I got back to the hotel it was too late. McQuay had done his dirty work."

He ran out of words then, which was fortunate. He didn't trust his voice to hold steady.

"I'm sorry," said Decker. "About your uncle, and about what I said. I knew you'd never do a dumb thing like buying a bogus treasure map."

Jake was surprised. He wondered if maybe the kid would turn out to be worth the trouble he'd caused.

They traveled quietly through the darkness at a steady pace. After a couple of hours, they topped a rise. This was something Jake would never have done in the daylight, and even at night it was risky. Still, he needed a vantage point where he could look over their back-trail. He could see a long distance in the moonlight, and far away something caught his attention. Decker saw it too, and touched his sleeve.

"Can it be?" he asked. "Or did I imagine it?"

"It can, and you didn't."

A flash of brightness had flared up miles away when someone had thrown fuel onto a hidden campfire.

"Do you think it's the outlaws?"

"Yeah. The Apaches wouldn't have pulled a dumb stunt like that."

"Then maybe we'd best get a move on."

It sounded like good advice to Jake. They headed out, still riding in the direction of the Mazatzal Mountains.

He recalled the old story that Nate had told him about how the ancient sailors had to make their way between the equally deadly Scylla and Charybdis. Jake was beginning to feel a kinship with those early adventurers. His own version of Scylla and Charybdis happened to be a band of cutthroat outlaws, and several bands of aggrieved Apaches.

"Things don't really look too good for us, do they?" said Decker.

"Cheer up," was his reply. "Think of it this way. At least you're not bored."

Chapter Three

Jake and Decker rode on through the night until it began to grow lighter in the east. They needed to find a place that would hide and shelter them. When they came upon a wash that ran slantwise between two hills, Jake could see that it had possibilities. He led the way down the wash until they were hidden from view.

"Looks like this is going to have to do," he said as he reined up.

He was aware of the risk they were taking by staying there. Thousands of tons of water could roar down a dry creek bed, without warning, from mountain sources that were miles away. But he was alert for weather formations over the high country, and there was no sign of a storm. The greater danger was being caught out in the open where they could be surrounded and killed.

He dismounted and looked around. Then he unloaded some of the gear they would need, and proceeded to ground-stake the mules and horses.

Decker followed along and awkwardly tried to help.

"Lockridge, I've been doing some thinking."

Jake glanced over at the kid who was standing near a mule's backside.

"Good," he said. "It never hurts to think once in awhile."

"Aren't you worried about showing me the location of your gold?"

Jake straightened up, took off his hat, and slapped the dust from it.

"Nope."

There was a look of disbelief on Decker's face.

"But I could rob you."

"You sure have a high opinion of your abilities."

Decker didn't seem to know how to take that, and so he let it pass.

"Well, you wouldn't have to worry about me at all if you were to make me your partner. Think about it. You're going to need help getting the stuff loaded and out of the mountains. Then there's sentry duty, and no telling what else. You need me, and it'll be worth your while to deal me in on this for a share."

Jake figured he should have seen it coming. But then, Decker had a point. Maybe he could actually be of some help. Then, too, if the kid was counting on part of the profit, he might be less troublesome.

"I suppose you want half," he said. "You're not going to get it."

"No. It's your treasure. All I'm doing is helping out and sharing the risk. I'll settle for a fifth, and I promise you won't regret it."

Jake doubted the part about not regretting it. But he wasn't greedy. It might be worth a fifth of the treasure to ensure Decker's cooperation.

"Okay," he agreed, "if you'll make yourself useful, you're in for a fifth of whatever we bring out."

Decker looked jubilant. Jake, on the other hand, was afraid that he'd just turned himself into six kinds of a fool.

By the time they'd settled in, it was fully daylight. Jake didn't know which he wanted more, a few hours of sleep or a cup of hot coffee. But the coffee was out of the question. There wasn't enough vegetation in the wash to filter the smoke of a campfire, and it wouldn't be wise to advertise their position. Instead, he settled for hardtack and jerky, which he shared with Decker. Afterward, he washed it down with a few swallows of water.

Without a "by your leave," Decker leaned against the side of the wash and closed his eyes, leaving the first watch to his new partner. Jake moved down the wash a few yards until he found a place where he could keep an eye on the gentle rise of ground to the east. It was from this direction that an Indian attack was likely to come.

He trusted the hill on the west side to shield them from the outlaws.

After a few hours, Jake had to struggle to keep alert. It was then that Decker suddenly opened his eyes and cleared his throat.

"You know, Lockridge, I've been thinking that maybe I should have stayed back home in Prescott."

Jake rubbed his eyes for they were watering from too much sun and too little sleep.

"You don't say. Isn't it a little late to be worrying about that now?"

"I had my reasons for leaving."

"Then you shouldn't beat yourself up about it," Jake advised. "Lots of older, wiser men than either of us have given in to temptation. Especially when that temptation was a goldmine."

Decker gave him a lopsided grin.

"That's a charitable viewpoint, but gold wasn't the real reason that I left home. That was just an excuse. The truth is, I didn't want to become a judge."

To Jake, the thought of Decker "sitting on the bench" judging others was outlandish, but he managed to keep from laughing.

"Afraid I didn't know that Prescott was so hard up for judges. No offense intended, of course."

Instead of being offended, Decker looked amused.

"No offense taken. Actually, the town has a pretty good one, right now. He's my grandfather, Jedidiah Kemp. The trouble is, Grandpa insisted that I read for the law, for he wanted me to become a judge, too. At least eventually. I hated the idea, so I kept finding other things to do with my time. The truth is, I was becoming an embarrassment to Grandpa. He couldn't stand it anymore. Just a few days before I left, he informed me that I had a 'glaring lack of ambition', and that I was 'jolly well going to show up at the law office each and every day and try to make something of myself'."

"So what did you do?"

"I gave in and suffered through a whole day in that stuffy little law office. Throughout all the time I was there, I kept picturing myself doing the same thing year after year. It made me sick. When I was able to shut the door of that place behind me, I went out and bought the map and a pack mule. Then I left a note for Grandpa, saddled my horse, and rode out of town as soon as it got dark."

Jake was surprised to find that he felt a good deal of sympathy for Decker. He felt some respect, too, for it took courage to do what he'd done. A man has the right to choose how he spends his life, but plenty of men have knuckled under to the kind of pressure that Decker's grandfather had applied. Even though he'd sneaked away at night, Decker was claiming his right as a free man. This was too important a decision for second thoughts.

"You can look at it this way," Jake said. "No matter what happens to you from now on, at least you're not sitting in a cramped office, ruining your eyesight by pouring through old law books."

The thought didn't seem to cheer him all that much.

"Considering the circumstances we're in, I may have lived a longer life if I'd stayed and done what Grandpa told me."

Jake eased his weight into a more comfortable position.

"Would you want to live for decades confined to law offices and court rooms?"

From the look on his face, the answer was obvious: "You've got a point, *amigo*," he said.

Jake yawned, and leaned back against the sloping side of the wash. Overhead, the sky was a clear shade of blue that grew lighter as it neared the horizon. The wind had stilled, and the morning air had a freshness about it. He admitted that it felt good to be in the middle of the desert wilderness, surrounded by the things of nature. There was no need for judges or lawyers out here. Here the strong and careful survived. Often luck played a part, too. But no question about it, this was a testing ground for the human spirit.

Jake wanted to drift off to sleep, leaving the kid to keep watch, but Decker wasn't going to let that happen, at least not right away.

"I've told you my story, Lockridge. Now, how about telling me yours?"

"There's not much to tell."

"What is it that you're running from? Aside from the outlaws, that is."

The question took him by surprise for Jake had

never run from anything in his life, and he proceeded to tell Decker so.

"I'm only here because my uncle sent for me. Before that, I was doing just fine. I was working on a big ranch in California."

"Did you ever want to get married?"

The question caught him off guard.

"Just once," he confessed.

"Then why didn't you?"

He wished he knew how to shut Decker up, but aside from knocking him in the head, it didn't seem possible. His life was a private matter, not a tale for storytelling. But he figured it would be easier to give in a little and satisfy Decker's curiosity.

"The woman in question wouldn't accept the likes of me, and I don't much blame her. All I had to offer was a cowpoke's wages and my homely face. The man she set her cap for was a banker who owned a sizeable chunk of California. They got married and moved into a big, fine house in Los Angeles."

It annoyed him to hear the bitterness in his voice for the past was done with. He hadn't seen Helen in almost a year, and it was time to forget the beautiful woman with raven hair and a smile that could make a man's head spin.

"I'm sorry about that," Decker sympathized. "But just so you'll know, your face doesn't look the way you seem to think it does. When you find the right woman, she'll like it well enough."

Surprisingly, Decker was trying to be kind to him, and Jake didn't know quite how to take it.

"I think losing your woman to that rich banker is probably why the gold is so important to you," he went on.

Maybe Decker was right, but Jake figured that a treasure in gold would be important to almost anyone, just because it was gold, and because of what it could do. Still, he wondered what might have happened if he could have offered Helen all of the things that great wealth could provide.

"Sorry to pry into your business," Decker apologized.

Jake accepted the apology with a nod, but he doubted if Decker was all that sorry.

He closed his eyes then, and slept. When he woke up a few hours later the sun was overhead. He felt rested, but he also felt uneasy.

"Have you seen or heard anything?" he asked Decker.

"No. Are you still worried about that campfire we saw?"

"I'd be a fool not to be worried. Somebody was out there. Stay here. I'm going to take a look around."

Jake made his way back down the wash. He wasn't concerned about being seen from the west, since the hill provided a screen. It was the east that served as a threat, for in the east were the Apaches. As planned, his dusty brown shirt and britches blended into the background as if they were a part of it. Still, he made sure to keep his head down. At last he reached the place where the wash angled to the southwest. This made him vulnerable from a different direction. He dropped to his belly and crawled onto the bank. From there, he inched his way forward, avoiding a sharp-needled cholla that was growing in his path. The sun was almost directly overhead, and its heat was bearing down. When he came to a spot that gave him an unobstructed view, he took out the field glasses. Shielding them so they wouldn't reflect sunlight, he peered into the distance.

It turned out that his uneasy feeling was justified. The outlaws were headed in the direction of the wash. He counted six in all, and they were leading extra mounts. With one quick motion, he stuffed the field glasses inside the pouch. Then he scrambled back up the wash to where his new partner was waiting.

His manner alerted Decker to the danger.

"Looks like you've got bad news," he said.

"Yeah. That light we saw last night didn't lie. Culebra and his bunch are headed this way. Looks like they're tracking us, and they'll be on top of us soon."

"Are we going to make a run for it?"

Jake's instincts were telling him to do just that, but his reason was telling him to stay put and make a stand.

"We can't run," he said. "If we do, we're apt to run into even worse trouble. No matter what we do the odds are against us. But our best chance is to hunker down and try to hold them off."

He noticed that Decker had a sickly look on his face. The kid was scared, and Jake didn't blame him. Truth to tell, he was scared too.

"Here, take my uncle's rifle," he said, handing him the Winchester that had been Nate's pride and joy. This was followed by the cartridges to go with it.

Jake grabbed his Spencer. His Colt was holstered, and he stuffed Nate's .45 inside his belt as well. They were far outnumbered, but at least they could do some damage to the outlaw gang.

"Come on," he said. "Those two hills form a pretty good barrier on either side. If they want us, they're going to have to ride down the middle. That's where you and I will be waiting for 'em."

They left the horses and mules where they were staked, while Jake grabbed one of the canteens and tossed another one to Decker. Then they made their way down the wash to the place where they would make their stand.

"Stay down," he warned Decker when they reached the spot between the two hills.

Here, by the side of the empty creek bed where it angled, was their only concealment and their only protection. The desert air was too dry for a man to sweat, but Jake was sweating anyway.

"I've change my mind," whispered Decker. "Reading for the law wasn't such a bad idea, after all."

Jake allowed that he had a point.

Quietly they waited, belly against the earthen side of the wash. Jake noticed that the kid seemed to be holding his breath. His own breath was shallow, and he could feel the blood pounding in his temples.

"Be patient," he warned Decker. "Wait until they get so close that you can't miss."

"You can count on me," he promised. "I've got a score to settle with that outfit."

As they drew closer, Jake could distinguish the one that was their leader. He looked like the sketch on the wanted dodger back in Arizona City. The only other outlaw he could put a name to, though, was Nettles. He ached to get McQuay in his sights, but had no idea which of the other four was Nate's killer. He steadied the Spencer, getting ready for the showdown. A second later, he saw a flash of moving color at the periphery of his vision. He turned his head and saw the advance of an Apache war party. Jake grabbed Decker's arm, just as he was getting ready to squeeze off a shot.

"Hold it," he ordered in a whisper.

Decker saw the war party then, and gasped.

More than a dozen braves were headed straight for the outlaws. They lay there, motionless, spectators to the drama that was unfolding before them.

Chapter Four

Culebra and his gang spotted the war party about the same time that Jake did, but it was too late for them to make a run for it. A fierce cry rent the air that made the hair on the back of Jake's neck stand up. Bursts of gunfire from Apache rifles followed, as the war party rushed the outlaws. Jake figured their rifles were Spencer Carbines like his own, and more than half the warriors were armed with them. There was no question about it, the gang was outnumbered and out-gunned. They realized it, too, for they were backing off, firing as they retreated. The Apaches, though, had no intention of letting them get away.

The desert air was filled with gun smoke, as well as a turbulence of dust stirred up by the horses. It was hard for Jake to see exactly what was going on. Still, he was able to make out one of Culebra's men, and he watched as his horse was shot out from under him. The unhorsed outlaw rolled backside-over-teakettle and came up firing. He was stilled by an Apache arrow. The remaining outlaws were taking refuge behind a tumble of rocks, leaving their horses to run free.

Jake was aware that if he and Decker hadn't been hidden in the wash, or if either of them had fired on Culebra's gang, they'd both be dead. Not that their prospects had been bright to begin with. As it was, the Apaches were taking care of a mutual enemy.

From behind the rock fortress, the outlaws were laying down a barrage of gunfire. It was taking a toll on the war party. Jake strained to see what was happening, and counted four Indian ponies without riders. Above the noise, he heard a scream. One of the outlaws had taken a hit. But so long as their ammunition held out, they could fend off the war party, killing them one by one. The Apaches must have come to the same conclusion. While Jake watched, they quickly and efficiently gathered their dead and retreated toward the mountains. As the small band passed close by them, neither Jake nor Decker moved a muscle. They were long gone before Decker laid his head on his arm and expelled his breath in a deep sigh.

"That was a close one," he said. "If I'd gone ahead and fired that rifle like I was going to, those Indians would have been right on top of us."

"Yeah. I've been thinking about that, myself."

"Do you think them outlaws will be after us again?"

Jake had been keeping watch on the rock spill where they were holed up.

"I think there's fewer of 'em now," he said. "Not to mention they're going to have to round up their horses—if they can."

"Well, that should slow them down anyway."

Jake lifted the canteen to his lips and took a swig of tepid water. It eased the dryness in his mouth.

"Slowing them down is about all it will do. They smell gold. Men have sold their souls for gold, so why should a few Apaches with carbines, or the likes of us, stop them from coming after it?"

"You haven't changed your mind about going up there?" Decker asked, nodding toward the mountains.

"Nope. That's what Nate intended to do before he was killed. I was his partner and now I'm his heir. My legacy is up there, and I'm going after it."

"I can understand you're wanting to do it. But I still think we're both crazy."

Jake figured that maybe he was right.

They made their way back to the animals where they would wait until nightfall.

Jake noticed that everything appeared to be more intense since their close call with death. The things that a man comes close to losing forever seem more precious, all of a sudden. Colors, sounds, and even smells were clearer and stronger. He had never before been more aware of the natural world around him.

It was clear that their narrow escape had affected Decker as well. Jake noticed that he'd been uncharacteristically quiet. He was acting like a man who had a lot on his mind.

At dusk they prepared to leave.

"Do you think that Culebra was one of the outlaws who was killed in the skirmish?" Decker asked.

"Nope. The Snake takes care of himself real well. I expect they'll regroup somewhere and be on our trail again before you know it."

"Mind telling me how you know he survived?"

"Sure. He was wearing a red shirt and riding a big *gruello*. The first outlaw who was killed, was wearing brown and riding a bay. The second one had on a dark shirt that didn't stand out either."

"Then I guess you couldn't be mistaken."

"I'm afraid not. If Culebra had died, we'd stand a better chance, for he's the brains of the outfit."

They rode down the wash for a short distance before they left it for higher ground. There was enough night light to ride by, and Jake was accustomed to night riding. He thought about how the desert was strange the way it changed from punishing heat in the daytime to bone-chilling cold once the sun slipped below the horizon. He stopped and took a minute to shrug into his coat. Decker borrowed the coat that had belonged to Nate.

Jake wished he were sitting beside a campfire, drinking hot coffee. But it was a fact of life that wishing never did a man much good.

Thankfully, there was no sign of their enemies, and the only noises were those that belonged. While they rode along together in silence, the night hours slipped by. After a time, Jake could smell moisture in the air.

"There's a river up ahead," he said.

This proved to be true, and they crossed the Verde River by moonlight after slaking their thirst and watering the horses and mules. Once they were across, they headed north. Jake's destination was a mountain in the Mazatzal Range. There would be a large peak to his right, and two others lay ahead in the distance. The closest of these was called Mazatzal Peak, and it was the first of Nate's landmarks.

Jake thought of his uncle and recalled how excited Nate had been about starting on this adventure. It was his nature to relish a challenge, and boredom was his greatest enemy. Only Nate and his pal, Gilley, would have risked riding into an Apache stronghold on a bet. And only Nate would have the knowhow, the pluck, and the good fortune to survive.

His uncle had told him the fantastic story right after he'd arrived in Arizona City. Nate and his friend had gotten lost, and soon after, Gilley had taken a bad fall.

"The old mountain goat went and lost his footing," Nate said. "He fell over the side, and I saw him go. It was all I could do to keep from hollering. I guess it happened so quick that Gilley didn't get a chance to holler either. It was a good thing, for we would've had Apaches swarming all over us. He landed on a narrow ledge below and laid there helpless. I grabbed a rope and lowered myself down. After I got Gilley off that ledge and back to a place where I could help him, it turned out that there wasn't anything I could do. I don't think he even knew that I was there."

Nate's voice broke when he got to the part about Gilley's death. He'd buried his friend in a shallow grave that he covered with stones. Afterward, he'd used all the tricks that he knew in order to avoid the small bands of Tontos that were moving through the mountains. He'd eked out what was left of his supplies, for he dared not attract attention by hunting. Always, he traveled by night and hid himself during the day.

He was looking for a place of shelter when he came upon a narrow crevice in the mountainside. After first checking for rattlers, he'd slipped inside. Toward the back, where it was so dark that he'd had to light a match, he discovered a lost treasure. There were old chests filled with coins and gold bars. By the looks of them, the chests had been hidden there for many years. No doubt the ones who'd stashed them were long dead. By this time, Nate had nothing left but one horse, so there was no way for him to bring it all out. Instead, he'd filled a bag with some of the coins, intending to return for the rest of the treasure. When he got to Arizona City, he'd sent word to Jake. He'd also sent his sister enough to keep her in comfort for years. The gold would enable her to quit her job at the hotel in Los Angeles, and to spend her time fixing up her own little house and tending her vegetable garden. Jake figured that if Nate's spirit was hovering around somewhere close, he'd have to be feeling a lot of satisfaction about that.

As for Jake, he was glad to be far away from California where Helen and her banker were living together in their big house. If anything good had come out of this journey, it was the satisfaction that he no longer yearned for the woman he couldn't have. In fact, he'd started thinking of her in a different light, and as a result, he almost felt sorry for the banker.

Decker broke into his thoughts with a question.

"Are you sure that you know where you're going?"

"I've got a good idea. I've spotted the first landmark already, and I'm on the lookout for the second one."

He'd caught Decker's interest.

"Since you've found the first one, how about the second landmark? Just what is it and where is it supposed to be?"

That was something Jake intended to keep to himself.

"Why don't you let me worry about the landmarks. I'll let you know when the time comes."

"Suit yourself," Decker said in a hurt voice. "But I thought we were partners."

Somehow, Decker always managed to rub him the wrong way.

"You can call us whatever you've a mind to. But I consider you to be a fellow who got himself into a peck of trouble, and who had to be rescued from his own foolishness. I was just as foolish in letting you talk me into a sizeable share of my treasure. But partners, we're not."

There was a long pause before Decker said anything.

"Suit yourself, Lockridge. Still, I don't understand you. We fought side by side back there, or at least we were ready and willing to fight. I'd have thought you'd have some trust in me by now."

Jake spoke before he could stop himself.

"Decker, you listen up. The last man in this world that I trusted is buried six feet under in a graveyard outside Arizona City. Right now, the only man I trust is myself."

His outburst was met with silence, and he began to regret the harshness of his words. Still, it was Nate who was supposed to be riding beside him, not this pampered young runaway. Besides, hadn't Decker jumped him from behind and tried to steal his horse? In this part of the country, a man had to prove himself worthy of trust, and Decker was still unproven.

They continued on through the night, depending on the darkness for cover. A cold wind arose, sweeping down from the northern peaks. Jake shivered in spite of the thickness of his coat. They were riding single file, and he was in the lead. This meant that he was heading straight into that cold wind with nothing to gentle its bite. It was going to be a long ride before sunrise brought any warmth.

Chapter Five

The constellations had moved across the sky and Jake was struggling to keep his eyes open. Suddenly he heard the sound of a horse blowing through its nostrils. Someone was out there in the darkness.

"Sounds like we've got company," Decker said in a low voice.

Jake reined up and drew the Spencer from its scabbard. They waited a moment in silence before he called out.

"Whoever you are, we've got you covered. Ride over here, easy like, with your hands in the air."

There was no answer. It didn't seem likely to Jake that one of the outlaws had broken away from the others to follow them. But someone was there, and he doubted if an Apache would have let himself be discovered.

"What do we do, now?" Decker asked.

Before Jake could come up with an answer, he had no need to. A riderless horse appeared from the shadows and trotted up to them.

"Hey, its dragging a lead rope," Decker said. "This must have been one of the outlaws' horses."

Jake had to agree. "It probably got separated from the others and took off in the same direction that we're heading."

Decker went closer to the horse and looked it over.

"This appears to be a fine animal. I wonder if it's the only one."

"Stay put, and I'll have a quick look around."

Jake rode out a short distance, searching the area, but he found nothing. It appeared that the horse had come alone.

"We'll take it with us," he said. "I expect we can use it when we start to pack out the gold."

"You think it'll take three pack animals?" Decker asked in awe.

"It might. I don't know since I haven't seen it first hand."

He added the lead rope to the others, and they moved on. Before they'd gone much farther, they began to ascend, leaving the desert behind. This time Decker was in front, leading the animals, while Jake followed, wiping out their trail as best he could. He figured that a skilled tracker would have little trouble following them, but Jake didn't want to make anything easy for his enemies.

Daylight found them sheltered beneath a rock over-hang that was high enough and deep enough to hide them and the animals, too. The front was hidden by a screen of palo verde trees and a few creosote bushes. They'd been so effective in concealing the hideout that Jake had almost passed it by.

He settled in, thankful for a place to hole up until night time. But Decker started complaining.

"You know, Lockridge, this business of getting rich isn't easy. In fact, sometimes it's downright uncom-fortable."

He was rubbing the circulation back into a foot that had gone to sleep on him.

"Yeah," said Jake, feigning sympathy. "Nothin's easy."

"I guess that's why so many people are dirt poor."

Jake figured that since Decker was a judge's grand-son, he knew very little about being poor, or about how hard a lot of folks struggled to make better lives for themselves and their families. He was getting fed up.

"Look, Decker, it was your own decision to leave the comfort of Prescott, not anyone else's, so quit your bellyaching. Besides, a few discomforts are a small price to pay in exchange for a fortune."

"You're right," he agreed. "I'm sure glad I teamed up with you, even if I'm not your partner. No doubt it was fate that you happened along when you did."

Jake made a rude noise and it startled his compan-ion.

"What's wrong, Lockridge? Don't tell me you don't believe in fate."

The kid had hit on a touchy subject.

"Maybe people have different notions about what the word means," he replied. "But if you think that 'fate' means we should all just sit back and watch while things happen to us, then I have no liking for it. As far as I'm concerned, a fellow has to take up the reins of his own life and guide it, himself. He has to make decisions and act on them. I figure that I'm responsible for all the mistakes that I make, and I can't blame fate or anything else. On the other hand, I'm due the credit when I don't make mistakes. Either way, as far as I'm concerned, fate can stay out of my business."

"You've got strong opinions, *amigo*, but how do you feel about luck?"

He wondered if Decker was trying to catch him up by throwing in a word that some folks thought was interchangeable with fate.

"I think that luck is something everyone's acquainted with, and I've known both good and bad. One or the other will come poking into a man's life every once in awhile, and he has to deal with it as best he can."

Decker appeared to chew on that for awhile.

"Tell me then," he said after a time. "Is squatting under this ledge like a couple of big ol' bullfrogs, good luck or bad luck?"

Jake chuckled in spite of himself.

"I reckon that it all depends on how you look at it. You're alive, and that's always good luck, especially in this neck of the woods."

All the while they were talking, Jake was scanning the slope across the valley. He watched as a red-tailed hawk searched for prey. Without warning, the large bird dived on powerful wings for a closer look at some creature it had spotted. The hawk was beautiful to watch, for it was a bird of grace and skill. Still, for one uncomfortable moment, Jake identified with its prey.

Throughout the day, he and Decker took turns keeping watch while the other slept. Jake's biggest concern was the Tonto Apaches who considered the Mazatzals to be their domain. When the outlaws regrouped, he wondered if they'd have the sand to enter this Apache stronghold. He knew that in spite of the danger, the lure of gold would be strong. Nobody could attest to that more than himself.

It occurred to him that Culebra and his men might decide to wait somewhere below and rob him on his way back to Phoenix. That would be easier and somewhat safer, and in their place that's what he would do. He decided that he'd have to find a different way off the mountain, even if he had to blaze the trail himself.

Shortly after dark, they left the shelter behind and quietly followed the curve of the mountain slope. Light from a full moon washed over the landscape, forcing them to keep to the shadows. However, it was that same bright light that enabled Jake to discover the next landmark. The instant he caught sight of it in the distance, he realized what it was, and his heart started pounding. A bluff had eroded in such a way as to display what looked like a roughly carved saguaro cactus in bas relief.

"Over there," he whispered to Decker, pointing toward it.

"What is it?"

"It's the second landmark. The one that you've been so curious about. See the wind-carved saguaro on the face of that bluff?"

"Well, I'll be . . ." he started when he spotted it. "It sure stands out, doesn't it?"

"It means that we're on the right track."

"You don't know how glad I am to hear that. I just want to collect that gold stash and get away from this place."

Jake felt exactly the same way, especially now that they were getting so close to the hiding place.

They continued along the narrow trail, single file. It was Jake's intention to cover as much ground as possible before daylight forced their withdrawal. But when daylight did begin to threaten, he was close to desperation. They were making their way across a narrow rock-strewn ledge. It was still too dark for him to see how far the drop-off was, but he knew it must be a long way down. He kept thinking of Gilley and how he'd died as the result of a fall. He also conjured up a mental picture of what the Apaches did to their enemies, and he knew they'd make sure that death took a long time coming. Fear won out against caution and pushed him to the point of recklessness. He knew they had to get off that ledge and find cover, and he hoped that Decker had plenty of nerve. As if he'd read Jake's thoughts, Decker called softly.

"Hey, slow down for Pete's sake."

Jake knew that a misstep could be fatal, but it would be just as fatal to be caught in the open in daylight. He compromised by slowing down, but only a little.

One step followed another, and it seemed to him that it was taking forever to get across the ledge. But, at last, they reached the other side. Jake didn't waste any time getting off the trail and into cover, after brushing out the most obvious signs of their passage.

At their present altitude, they were surrounded by Ponderosa pines, Arizona walnut, and a few syca-mores. They moved deep into the cover of the pines. Here Jake dismounted and stretched his weary mus-cles. Decker followed suit. All around them, millions of pine needles captured the morning breezes, and the music that resulted was pure pleasure to Jake's ears. He breathed deeply, filling his lungs with air, for no question about it, a pine forest smelled prettier than all of the fancy perfumes ever made.

Now that he no longer had to worry about being caught out in the open on that ledge, Jake started feel-ing an undercurrent of excitement. There was no doubt about it, they were getting close to their destination. He'd heard some of the old-timers in California talk-ing about how the sight of gold could make a man drunker than whiskey, and act just as foolishly. Jake couldn't say, first hand, if this was true, but if so, it was the kind of intoxication that he was eager to experience.

He pulled some jerky from a saddlebag and handed a piece to Decker.

"Hey, *amigo*," whispered Decker. "If I'm not being too nosey, just how many more landmarks do you have to find?"

Jake decided to answer his question.

"There's only one more."

He watched as Decker's face registered surprise in the early morning light. It was quickly replaced by eagerness.

"Look, we haven't seen so much as the shadow of an Indian since we entered the Mazatzals. Can't we risk riding a few more miles this morning?"

Jake held his anger in check.

"You sure forget things quick. How about that narrow miss we had with that bunch on the desert?"

Decker wasn't persuaded.

"That war party has got to be far to the south of us."

There wasn't any doubt about it. The kid had contracted a bad case of gold fever. It was making him reckless, and that could get them both killed.

"Forget it, Decker. We're not moving from here until nightfall. Only a fool would take off down that trail where he could be spotted for miles around."

It was plain that the order didn't set well. Jake

tensed, for it looked like he would have to physically stop Decker from going out there and giving them away. But the kid seemed to change his mind all of a sudden.

"You're the boss," he admitted. "And that treasure's not going anywhere."

They staked the animals, of which they now had five. Then they sprawled behind a screen of pine branches while they ate more of the jerky and finished the meal with pieces of dried apples.

"Hey, you don't really think that there's any Apaches around here, do you?" Decker started in again.

"I know for a fact that they're around."

"What makes you think so?"

Jake was inwardly cursing the ill fortune that had saddled him with an irritating greenhorn like Decker.

"Mostly all those unshod pony tracks that I spotted in the moonlight last night. They were on the same path that we took, and if the riders of those ponies used the trail, then it's a sure bet that other Apaches will follow."

Decker looked startled, and he lost his obstinance.

"Why didn't you say something before?" he demanded to know.

Jake shrugged. "No point in it. It would only have caused you unnecessary worry."

Decker gave him a lopsided grin.

"Well, we can't have that, now, can we?"

After that, they both settled down to wait out the

daylight. Jake could understand Decker's impatience. That same impatience was coursing through him, as well. But they would have to use common sense if they hoped to get out of the Mazatzals alive.

It was mid-morning when he heard the approach of horses. He signaled Decker to keep quiet, but it wasn't necessary for Decker had heard them, too. The kid was as motionless as a bronze statue. Jake wasn't sure he was even breathing. The fact was, Jake was holding his own breath.

From their place of concealment, they watched a dozen Apache braves ride single file down the trail. They were close enough to Jake that he could smell horse flesh. He took care not to look directly at them, for a man can sense when he's being watched. He hoped that Decker was aware of this too.

After what felt like an eternity, the last one passed on his way, never guessing that a couple of intruders hid close by. After allowing them time to get a lot farther down the trail, Jake breathed a prayer of thanks that one of the mules hadn't started braying the way they sometimes did. One of those wheezing, squeaking noises would have been the end of them.

"I've been acting like a dunce," Decker confessed when it was safe for him to speak. "I could have gotten us both killed."

Jake nearly choked on his own spit, for the kid's humility took him by surprise. A confession like that was something he'd never expected to hear.

They stayed concealed in the pines for the rest of

the day, waiting until it was safe to move out onto the trail once again.

"I've got mixed feelings about this," Decker said as they left their hiding place behind.

"I know what you mean. But I'm not going to turn tail and run. Not with a fortune in gold waiting for me."

The trail led northward, and they were climbing, little by little. They'd been in the saddle a couple of hours when they reached the final landmark. They'd been surrounded by a healthy stand of pines, when suddenly they came upon a wilderness of burned trees, victims of a forest fire. In the muted light, the shadows of leaning trunks and jagged stumps looked like a scene from a nightmare. The smell of ash still lingered. Those trees would never sing wind-songs again, nor would they spread their perfume over the mountainside. But Jake knew that this was Nature's way. The area would recover, and years from now, it would be as good as new.

He and Decker picked their way carefully through the desolation that served as Nate's last signpost. It was slow-going, and it was a long time before they found themselves among live trees again.

"That was it," Jake confessed.

"That was what?" asked Decker.

"The last landmark that Nate told me to look for."

"Then we're close, for sure."

"Should be."

Jake recalled the instructions that Nate had given on

their first night back in Arizona City, and he knew that
he and Decker had almost reached their destination.

"Wait here," he ordered.

"Why? Where are you going?"

"On ahead, by myself. I'm looking for something
that won't be easy to find. When I do, I'll come back
for you."

To his surprise, Decker didn't argue.

Jake rode alone on the final leg of his journey. It
took awhile, but at last he found what he was searching for. It was a narrow, almost invisible opening in
the mountain. When he caught his first glimpse of it
in the moonlight, his heart started pounding like a tom-
tom. He sat in the saddle looking at it for a minute,
then he rode back and fetched Decker.

When Decker saw the crevice he seemed awed.

"So this is the hiding place," he whispered.

Jake knew how he felt. Until now, the treasure story
must have seemed like a tall tale. A lot of the time, it
had seemed that way to him, and he'd had the advantage of seeing and handling some of those strange gold
coins.

"Come on, Decker, we'll picket the animals back in
those trees where they can't be seen. Then we'll climb
up to the crevice so we can be hidden inside before
daylight."

"My friend, you're not going to believe this,"
Decker said. "But my hands are shaking."

Jake believed it, for his hands were shaking too.

Chapter Six

Jake and Decker sat near the entrance of the cave, just far enough back to be hidden. It was here they waited for daylight, but their patience was wearing thin.

"I can't stand this any longer," Decker complained. "Here I am close to a fortune in gold, and I can't even go back there and touch it, let alone see it."

"My uncle warned me that the floor of the cave is rough. You could fall and break your neck. That's not to mention the possibility of disturbing some unfriendly snakes."

The threat of snakes settled him down a little, and Jake closed his eyes and tried to doze off. It had been a long ride and he needed rest for the work that lay ahead. But sleep eluded him. Every nerve in his body was tense with anticipation. Decker wasn't the only one who wanted to go back and heft those gold bars. He imagined how beautiful they would be bathed in sunlight. But no matter, he was going to have to wait. If they were to light a lantern, or even a candle, it would light up the mouth of the cave for anyone who happened to be in the vicinity. The minutes seemed to crawl until, at last, the sun came up, pouring its brightness into the opening.

"Are you ready?" Decker asked, getting to his feet.

"As ready as I'll ever be. Let's go find it."

Jake led the way toward the back. The cave was narrow, but it was a lot deeper than he expected. Soon, light from outside no longer illuminated it. He took one of the fat candles from his pack that he'd put there in case they were needed. Next, he fumbled with the match box, nearly dropping it in his haste. At last, he was able to pull out a match and strike it. Then he touched it to the wick. A yellow flame flickered to life and cast shadows along the rock walls. He no longer worried about the light being spotted from outside, for they were far too deep within the mountain.

With the candle held in front of him, Jake searched for signs of the treasure.

"Please don't tell me that someone has gone and beat us to it," Decker muttered.

Jake didn't think it was likely. Carefully he made his way farther back. But soon both the sides and the top started closing in, forming a tunnel. The space became so small that Jake had to crouch in order to go on. After a few more yards, he spotted a dark heap piled against the back wall.

"This has to be it," he told Decker.

After first checking for rattlers, Jake reached down and pulled back an old buffalo robe. Beneath it, he found three leather bound chests. The chests had been pried open, and Jake figured this was where Nate had found his gold. He tried to keep his hand steady as he lifted the lid of the nearest chest and pushed it back.

Decker was looking over his shoulder, and he heard the kid gasp, or maybe he'd gasped himself. In the dim light of a single candle, the golden bars gleamed. There weren't any coins in the first chest, though, and he guessed those were the ones that Nate had taken because they were smaller and easier to pack out than the bars. The other two chests were filled with both bars and coins.

"Come on," said Jake. "Let's get this stuff loaded into the burlap bags and stacked by the entrance. Then, come dark, we'll bring the mules and the horses up."

Jake melted some wax and stuck the candle against one wall. Then he lit another and did the same thing. Decker fetched the bags and they set to work. It was awkward in the dim, cramped quarters, but Jake wasn't about to complain, and for once, Decker wasn't complaining either.

Jake's knees and thighs were aching by the time they'd emptied the chests and had the treasure transferred to the bags. Decker reached over and lifted one end of the heavy old buffalo robe.

"I wonder who this belonged to?" he asked. "This robe and the gold?"

"I've done some thinking about that, myself," Jake confessed. "That stuff has been here a long time, from the looks of it. Nate thought that some of the early explorers from Mexico might have stashed it here for safekeeping. But I guess we'll never know for sure."

Decker smoothed and folded the woolly hide as best he could in their cramped quarters.

"Unless you want this, I'd kind of like to have it," he said.

"Welcome to it."

It was the last thing that was dragged from the back of the cave.

Again, Jake found himself waiting for it to get dark. But even though they were eager to start, he and Decker were both tired and needed sleep. The remaining daylight hours would be a respite. Decker bedded down on the buffalo robe, while Jake leaned against the stone wall, softened only by his coat. He doubted if he would actually fall asleep, but if he did, he would sleep lightly. When he did doze off, he dreamed of Nate, a faceless killer, and a sky that rained gold coins. It was twilight when he awakened.

Shortly after nightfall, Jake made his way down the slope to bring up the animals. On the way, he acknowledged the uneasy feeling that he was having about Decker. It was true that the kid had behaved himself since that attack the day they met, but he'd had the promise of gold to secure his cooperation.

Now, with the gold discovered and packed on the animals, Decker might decide that having it all would be
better than settling for a fifth. Jake decided that it
would be wise not to be over-trusting. Besides worrying about Decker, he was going to have the outlaws
to deal with if he succeeded in getting off the mountain.

Decker was waiting for him and eager to help him
get the animals loaded. They needed to get through
the burned-off area of the forest and find cover before
sunup. After that, there was the long, narrow ledge to
contend with.

"Go on ahead with the mules," Jake said. "And I'll
follow with the horse."

He figured that way he could keep an eye on Decker
and not have to turn his back on someone he didn't
trust.

"Sure," the kid replied.

They started down the steep slope and headed back
the way they'd come. They weren't going all the way
to the base of the mountain, though. Jake had already
made the decision to find a different route.

They passed through the ghostly graveyard of trees
without incident, although it gave him an eerie feeling.
If Decker felt the same uneasiness, he kept it to himself. When they stopped to make camp and hide themselves throughout the day, they were near to the ledge
again. He wondered how Nate would have been feeling now, had he been able to go on this expedition as
he'd planned to do. Jake couldn't think about the gold

without thinking about his uncle and the injustice that was done. Now that he knew the name of Nate's killer, he was going to see that he was hanged or shot. That is, if he hadn't died in that skirmish with the Tontos. While he couldn't explain it, Jake had a feeling that McQuay was still alive.

When it came time for them to head out, Decker took the lead without a word. Carefully, they made their way across the ledge of earth that stood between them and their escape from the Apache stronghold. Jake was satisfied that he'd taken every precaution to avoid capture, yet luck had been on their side too. Luck wasn't something he ever counted on, but he gratefully welcomed its presence.

Once they were safely on the other side, he felt a sense of relief. But it was short-lived. He had to find another way off the mountain. There was at least one, but he was loathe to use it. It was an ancient trail that he'd noticed on the way up. It branched off into the wilderness, and he had no idea where it came out. It could lead to an Apache camp, or it could leave them lost and stranded in the midst of nowhere. Still, the unknown was preferable to walking into the arms of Culebra and his cutthroats.

When they came to the trail, Jake called softly to Decker who'd gone on past it.

"This way," he said.

Decker hesitated. "Do you think that's a good idea?"

"Unless you want to turn that gold over to the out-laws."

"You've got a point, but we don't know where this trail will take us."

"Then I guess we'll just have to find out. How about taking the lead?"

Decker didn't move.

"Look, Lockridge, I know you don't trust me, especially since we found the gold, but you'd better start. Whenever you dropped off to sleep, I could have caved your head in with a rock and nobody would have been the wiser. Then I could have taken off with everything. You may have noticed that I didn't. What I've tried to do is earn my one-fifth share. I owe you my life, for goodness sake."

His speech was heartfelt, and Jake was a little ashamed of his distrust. Without a word, he took the lead down the narrow old pathway with a silent prayer that it wouldn't lead them astray.

Here the trees grew thick, shutting out much of the nightlight and leaving their path in darkness. Jake lost his sense of time. He had the strange feeling that he was moving slowly through a dream. Then, without warning, the trail altered its direction. According to Jake's calculation, they were headed due south.

It wasn't long before the dun's ears perked up. It picked up its pace as the other animals had done. They smelled water. Soon they arrived at a creek that was fed by run-off from the peaks. Jake called a halt while the animals drank their fill. They'd been on short rations for a long time. He and Decker drank and filled the canteens as well.

"We'd better get moving," Jake said when they'd finished. "The juncture of a trail and a creek is apt to be a popular spot."

They mounted up and continued to ride throughout the rest of the night.

It was turning out that Jake's decision had been a good one. The trail hadn't gotten them into the trouble that it might have—at least it hadn't yet.

After another day of hiding and a night of riding, they descended to the banks of the Verde River. He reckoned their location was far to the south of the place where they'd begun their ascent. The other trail would be where the outlaws waited. How long they'd wait was a question that Jake couldn't answer.

"If Culebra and his outfit should decide to backtrack, what are we going to do?" Decker said.

"The best we can, I reckon."

Decker didn't appear to be reassured.

"What are you going to do about this McQuay fellow who killed your uncle?"

McQuay was always at the center of Jake's thoughts.

"I expect he'll be along with the others. When I meet up with him, I'll either shoot him or take him back to Arizona City to be hung. Nate always set great store in doing things the proper way, so it's better if he hangs. But either way, I'll be satisfied. And I'm not forgetting Nettles either. I want him too."

They were near the river's edge by this time. Jake reined up and dismounted. This was a chance to rest and let the horses and mules have a drink. While Decker led the animals to the water, he stood back a ways from the embankment, watching and listening for any motion or sound that was out of place. All the while, he was burdened with the strange feeling that he was the one who was being watched. Off to the side, he heard a rustling in the brush near a cotton-wood. He peered into the darkness, but saw nothing. It might simply have been a nocturnal creature who'd been startled by their presence, but Jake couldn't take the chance. The outlaws may have hedged their bets and posted someone to watch for him. Decker, who was several yards away, appeared to be unaware that anything was suspicious. Jake's hand slid toward his revolver, but before he could draw, a shadowy figure emerged, and he had a gun pointed at Jake's vitals.

"Put your hands up *hombres*!" the figure ordered.

The voice was youthful, and the youth was scared. Jake did as he was told. So did Decker, and Decker wasn't even in the line of fire. One thing for sure, the scared kid who was holding the gun on him wasn't one of Culebra's hardened criminals. Just maybe they had a chance.

Chapter Seven

A few long seconds passed before the young gunman called out to his companion.

"Alicia, you can come out, now. I've got them covered."

While Jake watched, a woman emerged from deep shadows. She was leading two horses. He tried to catch a glimpse of her face, but in addition to the darkness, a shawl partially covered her features. He was able to tell by the graceful way she carried herself, though, that she, too, was young.

"Over here, *mi hermana*," the gunman ordered.

His sister obeyed.

"Look," Jake said in his most persuasive voice, "I don't know who you are, or who you think we are, but we don't mean you any harm."

"That remains to be seen, *Señor*." the young woman

replied in the same accented English that her brother had spoken. "Keep them covered, Miguel."

It had been useless appealing to her. All Jake could do was stand there helpless, looking down the business end of a gun, while she efficiently disarmed him.

"Your pack animals are burdened," she observed. "What cargo could you be bringing from the mountains?"

Jake felt like swearing. He and Decker had gotten all this way in spite of Apaches and outlaws, only to be robbed by a woman and her kid brother.

"Just some rocks for my aunt's new flower garden," he replied flippantly.

Her brother scoffed at his answer.

"Search their packs, Alicia," he commanded.

Jake waited helplessly while she walked over and pulled open one of the burlap bags. A gold bar fell into her hand. In the moonlight there was no mistaking it for what it was, and she drew in her breath sharply.

"*Madre de Dios*," she exclaimed.

"What is it?" her brother demanded to know.

"Gold. They're carrying bags of gold bars."

"Make sure," he said. "Search the other sacks."

While the woman named Alicia was busy with her task, Miguel's attention was drawn to her and the sacks of gold. Jake decided it was time to act. Without warning, he flung himself across the distance that separated him from his enemy. He grabbed Miguel's wrist, twisting it until he yelped in pain. The gun fell to the ground. Jake shoved him backward and scooped up the weapon. He pointed it at Miguel who was struggling to regain his balance.

"Hold it right there!" Jake ordered.

As soon as he'd made his move, Decker ran and grabbed the woman. He held her tight while she kicked and struggled.

"Lie face down on the ground," Jake ordered Miguel.

"Don't you dare hurt my sister, or I will find a way to kill you," he threatened.

"It's not my intention to hurt your sister."

While keeping an eye on his grounded attacker, Jake cut strips of burlap. First, he bound Miguel's wrists, then he went over and bound Alicia's.

"How dare you treat us this way!" she protested.

Jake had just about had his fill.

"Now, how do you expect us to treat you? You hold us at gunpoint and try to rob us of our gold, not to mention the horses and mules. We're lucky that you didn't shoot us. Back where I come from, *Señorita,* that kind of behavior is frowned on."

She turned into a bundle of fury before Jake's eyes.

"You lie!" she spat. "We do not steal. And we only kill those who need killing."

"Well, you sure fooled me. Just what were you planning to do, then?"

"We were curious, that's all, about you and your cargo. We're quite harmless."

Jake didn't doubt the part about the two being curious, but he'd believe they were harmless on the day that rattlesnakes lost their venom.

"My sister is telling the truth," Miguel protested. "You've got no right to hold us against our will."

"That's not the way I see it," said Jake as he holstered his revolver and handed the confiscated one to Decker. "You held my partner and me against our will, so you've got no call to complain."

The young woman twisted away from Decker's hold and came to stand directly in front of Jake.

"Miguel and I were both hasty, and I apologize. If you let us go, *Señor*, I promise that you'll never see us again."

That was all he needed, Jake thought. Two more enemies who were eager to bushwhack him for the gold. As if he didn't have enough trouble already.

They were both young. The boy couldn't have been more than sixteen. His sister was possibly a couple of years older.

"What are you two doing out here by yourselves, anyway?" he asked.

"What we were doing is none of your business," said Miguel, who was struggling with his burlap bindings.

Jake was losing patience.

"Fine," he said, "if that's the way you want it. But you have to know that those mountains and this whole area is crawling with Apaches, and they don't treat trespassers kindly. If that's not enough to make you worry, there's a gang of outlaws after the gold in those bags, and they'll do anything to get it. Whatever the reason you're here, it's not worth the risk."

All the defiance went out of Alicia then.

"What is going to happen to us?"

Miguel stepped to her side and tried to comfort her.

"Don't be afraid, *mi hermana*, even men such as these won't hurt you, and they won't want to drag us along with them. They'll have to let us go."

Jake bit back a sharp reply, although he was weary of being burdened with greenhorn kids and their bad tempers.

"You'd better hope that we decide to take you with us," he said when he had control of his tongue. "If we don't, you may soon find yourselves at the ungentle mercy of Culebra and his outfit."

"Culebra!" said Miguel. "He's an animal."

It appeared to Jake that he'd finally gotten through to him. He'd gotten through to his sister as well.

"We'll willingly go with you," she said. "My brother and I won't give you any more trouble. Is that not true, Miguel?"

Jake could tell that Miguel wasn't happy about the arrangement, but the kid's survival instincts kicked in and he promised to cooperate. Jake nodded to Decker, who untied their hands.

"We'll keep your weapons, for now," Jake told them.

Miguel started to protest, but Alicia raised her hand to shut him up.

"Where were you headed?" Jake asked, wondering if he'd get a straight answer.

"We were on our way to Hermosillo," she said.

"Isn't that down on the Sonora River in Mexico?" Decker asked.

"*Si.* My father has friends there who will take us in."

"What happened to your father?"

"He was killed up in those mountains by Apaches. You see, he, too, was searching for the yellow metal."

Jake figured that since no one else knew of the ancient stash of gold, the search that Alicia was talking about involved prospecting.

"Where were you when he was killed?" he asked.

"Papa had me and Miguel hidden away in a cave. He'd go out alone, so we didn't even know when he was attacked, only that he didn't come back for us."

Her voice broke, but she pulled herself together quickly.

"We went out to search for him. We found his remains and buried them."

Jake didn't even want to picture in his mind what they'd found to bury.

"I'm sorry," he said, realizing how puny those words sounded in light of what had happened to them.

"What about your mother?" Decker asked.

"She died a long time ago. Papa was all that we had."

The way Jake sized it up, those two were in a bad way. They were alone in the world without any resources. In addition, they were in the same danger from Culebra's outlaws and hostile Apaches as Decker and himself. He still didn't trust them, though, and he figured if they could get their hands on his gold, they'd be off like a shot. Still, he could see them safely to a town, or at least he could try.

"Look, we can't stay here any longer," he said. "No telling when that gang will get tired of waiting and start backtracking. You two mount up and you can ride with us as far as Phoenix. You should be safe there."

Instead of gratitude, he got anger, at least from Miguel.

"We don't need your help, *gringo*. The Sandovals can take care of themselves."

"Then take care of yourself and your sister by being sensible."

"He's right, Miguel," Alicia pleaded. "We would be safer with them than we would be alone."

Grudgingly, Miguel conceded.

They all got on their horses and crossed the river. Jake took care to go last, so he could keep watch on the others. He recalled how deeply he'd distrusted Decker, but now, Decker was the one he was relying on. Life was full of surprises.

There was little time left of darkness, but Jake and the others made the most of it. In the pre-dawn grayness, they were concealed in a draw, much like the one that had sheltered them during the skirmish. This didn't please Miguel.

"You've got us hiding in here like a bunch of prairie dogs, and that's not fitting," he complained to Jake.

"As I recall, your father had you hiding in a cave. What's the difference?"

Miguel let loose with a string of Spanish that Jake was certain was unfit for Alicia Sandoval's ears.

"Maybe it's not fitting for a man to hide but it's a lot worse to be killed and robbed," Jake said. "I want to live through today, and I want to live through a lot of other days as well. If I have to fight, I'll fight. If I have to hide, I'll hide."

Alicia drew her shawl more tightly around her slender figure.

"Stop complaining, *mi hermano*," she scolded. "These men are right. We have to do what we must in order to survive."

Miguel's attitude remained arrogant and surly, but he minded his sister and kept quiet. That quiet was a relief to Jake's ears.

They were all tired and hungry, so Jake and Decker shared their food with the Sandovals. All the while, Jake was alert for any sign of the enemy.

"If you want, I'll take the first watch," Decker offered after they'd finished eating.

Jake wasn't sure if it was during that moment of confrontation at the turn-off that he'd begun to trust his partner, or if the trust had grown slowly and subtly. What he did know was that he trusted Decker now, more than he trusted any other man alive. He also admitted to himself that Decker was, indeed, his partner. You couldn't share the same hardships and dangers for that long a time and not become partners in the true sense.

"Thanks for the offer but I'll take the first watch," he answered. "You try and get some sleep."

He didn't have to say it outright. Decker was aware that the two of them would have to keep constant watch on the Sandovals, as well as stay on the lookout for the outlaws.

He kept the Spencer at hand, and his revolver was strapped at his side. Besides that, he had Nate's Colt .45, and Alicia Sandoval's shotgun. Decker had Nate's Winchester and the Colt that young Sandoval had pointed at Jake.

It didn't take long for the others to bed down, and Decker was soon snoring. The day lightened with the sunrise, and Jake stretched his cramped, aching muscles. He was surprised to look up and see Alicia approaching him. She still clutched her shawl around her, but he could see her face clearly now. She had large, dark eyes, a high forehead, and luminous skin, in spite of living in the sun-baked, wind-blown desert. When she looked at him, Jake thought of the old saying that the eyes were the mirrors of the soul. If that were true, he thought, then Alicia Sandoval must be close kin to an angel. It was hard for him to believe, looking at her that way, that she would ever have stolen his gold, or allowed her brother to do so.

"You want to talk to me about something?" he asked.

She stopped a few feet away from him.

"Trouble is coming. I can feel it."

"Well, Ma'am," he said, "I don't need any special powers to tell me that."

Worry etched her face.

"But you don't understand. I feel that danger is very close."

"Better listen to her, Lockridge," called Miguel. "Alicia has a way about her. A lot of times, she can feel things before they happen."

Looking into those mysterious eyes of hers, Jake believed him.

"There's something you should know," she said. "Not far from this place is an abandoned adobe *casa*. We took refuge there with my father when we were on our way to the mountains. If we hurry, we might be able to reach it before trouble catches up to us."

Jake knew that she was frightened, and that she thought the abandoned house would offer more protection, but he didn't relish leaving what cover they had and striking out across open country in search of a place that might well be somewhere else.

"It wouldn't be a good idea to leave here just now," he said. "If we failed to find the house in time, we'd be caught out in the open. Then, too, if we were to find it, we could be easily trapped inside, for once it was surrounded by Apaches or outlaws, there wouldn't be a way out for us."

"I hate to admit it, but he's right," said Miguel,

who'd continued to listen. "That place could turn into a death trap."

Jake was surprised to hear Miguel agreeing with him on anything. At the same time, it pained him to see Alicia's shoulders sag in hopelessness.

"I'm afraid we're going to die here in this wash," she said.

"I'll do my best to see that we don't." It was the only promise he could make.

She went back to lie down beside her brother, while Jake turned his attention to the north, the direction from which an attack from the outlaws would come. He didn't have to wait long.

In the distance, he saw a dust cloud moving in their direction. It appeared that Culebra and his gang had grown tired of waiting. Jake grabbed the Spencer and called out to Decker.

"Wake up, they're coming!"

Decker scrambled to the edge of the wash. The Sandovals joined them.

"My gun, *por favor*. You need all the help you can get, and I must protect my sister, as well as myself."

He had a point.

"Give Sandoval his gun," he ordered Decker. "And you take Nate's revolver."

"I will take my shotgun," Alicia said.

The four of them leaned against the side of the wash, watching the dust cloud draw closer. Jake could feel the blood pounding in his temples as he waited to have Nate's killer in his sights. The bad thing was, Culebra was going to have Jake in his.

Chapter Eight

Jake was able to make out the outlaws' faces now. Nettles was riding a dark horse with a blaze. Culebra was on his *gruello*. He didn't recognize the others, but unless McQuay had been killed in that set-to with the Apaches, he was among them. The outlaws hadn't spotted them yet, as they were well-hidden in the wash, but Jake had no doubt that they were looking for him, and for the treasure that he carried.

"Stay down and hold your fire until they're almost on top of us," he ordered. "I'll give the signal."

He was counting on surprise to give them the advantage, and the fact that they couldn't miss from close range.

Jake was readying the Spencer when the sound of gunfire ripped through the stillness. Miguel had disobeyed his order and had fired a wild shot into the midst of the outlaws. Warned, the gang scattered like geese in a lightening storm. Jake heard Culebra shout an order to his men.

"Get them! Don't let them live!"

The outlaws began firing in their direction. Jake shoved Alicia down in the wash to protect her and fired the Spencer at the nearest target. Decker and Miguel were helping to hold the outlaws back, and the air was filled with the smell of gunsmoke. Jake knew the best strategy was to take out the leader, so he set his sights on Culebra. But as he leaned forward to squeeze off a shot, he felt something slam into his arm. His aim was spoiled, and the *gruello* carried its rider out of harm's way.

Jake could actually taste his frustration. He tried to target the outlaw again, but Culebra was on the move, now, often placing the *gruello* between himself and his enemies. Jake noticed that one of Culebra's men had fallen from his saddle and was crawling along the ground, trying to make himself less of a target.

The Snake was the kind of man who liked to have the advantage, and in this instance the advantage was clearly not his. He'd been attacked when he wasn't expecting it, and his enemy was well-armed and well-supplied. Their numbers were also equal. In addition, one of his men was on the ground, and another was wounded. He gave the order to retreat. Those on horseback withdrew, leaving their grounded partner behind.

As soon as the abandoned outlaw realized his predicament, he shouted a curse at Culebra's back. Jake noticed that for all the good it did him, he might as well have turned and spit in the wind.

"Toss your gun away!" he shouted. "We've got you covered."

The outlaw looked around desperately. Jake was afraid that he'd go crazy and start shooting. But sanity prevailed.

"Don't shoot!" he yelled. "I'm throwing it away."

He slid the gun away from him, and it skidded a few yards over the rough ground.

"All right, get to your feet," Jake ordered.

He slowly obeyed, keeping his hands in the air.

Decker was the one who climbed out of the wash and brought him back. It was a good thing, for Jake was having trouble keeping his balance. His sleeve felt wet, and he looked down to find that it was soaked in blood. His arm was numb where the bullet had entered, but he doubted if the numbness would last.

"Tie his hands," Jake ordered.

Miguel took a strip of leather from his pack and bound the outlaw, while Decker kept him covered.

"I'm real glad to see this *hombre*," Decker said. "He's one of them that robbed me, and the gun he's carrying was given to me by my grandfather."

"Then it's good that you got it back," Miguel said.

"Is he the one that's wearing your boots?" Jake asked.

"No such luck."

Jake struggled to focus, for voices were becoming distant and blurred.

"Now that I've studied on it, I recall seeing you in Prescott," said Decker to the outlaw. "You appeared before my grandfather, Judge Kemp, a few years back."

"What of it?"

"What had he done?" Alicia asked.

"It seems he robbed some settlers, and he pistol-whipped one of them. He ended up spending some time in jail."

"Yeah, I remember that judge," said the outlaw. "Somebody ought to do something about that self-righteous old geezer. He preached at me 'til my ears went to sleep."

Decker grinned.

"That's Grandpa all right, and you're Amos Farley."

Jake didn't hear whether or not Farley acknowledged his name, for he slipped to the ground, unconscious.

The next thing he was aware of was a stabbing pain in his arm. He found himself lying against soft, sunshine-scented hair.

"We must stop the bleeding," he heard Alicia say.

He felt his wound being cleaned and packed. His mouth was dry and he tried to ask for water. She held a canteen to his lips and gently helped him to drink.

"We have to get out of here *pronto*," said Decker. "For one thing they're apt to be coming back to get Farley, and for another that gunfire alerted half the

Territory. We could have Apaches on top of us any time now."

Jake understood the danger but he simply didn't have the strength to get up and do anything about it.

"Go ahead, Decker," he said. "You're in charge, now."

"Let's get him on his horse," was his partner's first order.

Jake felt Alicia's arm around his waist, steadying him as he tried to stand. He noticed that Miguel had picked up the carbine that had slipped from his hands. Only Decker stood between the Sandovals and his gold, and he didn't think Decker would have a chance if they decided to grab it and make a run for it.

A moan escaped him as he was boosted into the saddle. But once there, he was able to stay in place.

"Hey, what are we going to do with Farley?" Decker asked. "Unless someone rides double, we don't have a horse for him."

"Let him walk," said Miguel. "It's a fine day for it. Not a cloud in the sky."

"Oh no you don't." Farley protested. "You ain't going to make me walk across this desert."

"Funny, that's what you made me do, and one of you stole my boots and left me without water," said Decker.

Farley decided not to press his luck.

The others mounted up, and someone took the lead ropes.

"Get moving, *hombre*," Miguel ordered the outlaw.

It took all of Jake's remaining strength and willpower to keep from falling off, but they headed out of the wash, with Farley on foot. Where they were going, he didn't know.

"Do you think the outlaws will be coming after us soon?" Alicia asked.

"You can bet on it, Miss," Farley said. "If you don't think Culebra cares anything about rescuing one of his men, you can bet that he cares about rescuing that gold. Besides that, McQuay ain't too fond of Lockridge, and that goes double for Nettles. Nettles figures he's got a score to settle."

Jake recalled the outlaw's expression when he'd called his bluff at the poker game. He knew that to Nettles' way of thinking, he'd made a fool of him in front of everyone in the Oasis that night. That kind of humiliation was hard for someone like Nettles to forget.

Jake was lightheaded and his mouth felt as dry as a sandstorm. Then he must have dozed off, for the next thing he knew Alicia was seated on the dun behind him with her arms around him to hold him steady.

"We've got to get him to shelter right away," he heard her say.

"That old adobe *casa* shouldn't be far from here," Miguel reminded her.

After that, their voices grew dim. All Jake was aware of was the rhythmic gait of the horse beneath him and the fire that burned in his left arm.

It was an eternity later that he felt himself being

lifted and carried. Then he was lowered onto blankets. It was cold, as cold as he ever remembered it being. He couldn't stop himself from shivering. Then he smelled buffalo hide as the old robe was spread over him. Afterward, he felt a little warmer. Someone built a fire close by, and this helped even more. Then the darkness closed over him.

As it began to recede, he heard the murmur of voices. The pain in his arm was intense, and his face was bathed in sweat. He fought to kick the covers off.

"There, it's done," he heard Alicia say.

Jake struggled to open his eyes, and when he did, he saw her standing over him. There was a knife in her hand. She must have seen the alarm in his eyes, for she talked to him softly.

"Do not worry. I used this knife to cauterize your wound after I removed the bullet. If you can avoid infection, I think you'll be alright. It's fortunate that you'd passed out."

Knowing the procedure well, and having done it once himself, he agreed with her.

He attempted to form the words, "thank you", and she seemed to know what he was trying to say.

"You must rest, now, Jake, and try to regain your strength."

His mouth was even drier than before, and he desperately wanted a drink. But before he could ask, Decker was holding a cup of water to his lips. It had been dipped from the Verde River, it was lukewarm, and it was better than anything he'd ever tasted.

"Where are we?" he asked after he'd drained the cup.

"We're in that old house that the Sandovals told us about. We had to get you to shelter so Alicia could pull that bullet out of you."

Jake knew they'd done what they had to but he worried about their vulnerable position.

"Keep a close watch on Farley," he whispered.

"Consider it done, *amigo*."

Jake laid back and closed his eyes. He'd always been a loner, except for his time with Nate, and they'd been separated for years until their meeting in Arizona City. Mostly, he liked it that way. He'd learned to depend on himself. But now he was forced to depend on others, and Decker and the Sandovals were a surprise. It seemed to him that Decker had changed a lot since their association had begun. He'd matured and become responsible. But Jake was also seeing the Sandovals in a different light, at least he was seeing Alicia differently.

He slept then. He dreamed that he was covered in a dozen blankets, and he fought to throw them off. From time to time, he felt the relief of a cool cloth being applied to his forehead. Then, at last, he slept without dreams.

Chapter Nine

Alicia Sandoval stepped to the doorway for a breath of air. Inside the cramped room it was stifling. But the one called Decker had built a fire because the big *gringo* was suffering from a chill, and besides, they'd needed the fire to heat the knife. After she'd probed for the bullet, the wound had to be burned. She'd done such a thing before, once assisting her father, and once alone, but it was never easy.

Alicia couldn't forget how Jake Lockridge had pushed her down in that wash and shielded her from gunfire with his own body. This had been an act of gallantry that she hadn't expected.

In the west, the sun was sinking below the horizon, and soon the desert would cool. This had always been a welcome time. It was the time that her father would be resting from his labors and enjoying the company of his children. She felt a dull ache in her heart as she thought of him. She'd pleaded with him not to go into those mountains to prospect for she'd heard how dangerous they were. But he'd ignored her words and now he was dead. In fact, she and Miguel were lucky to be alive themselves. She recalled what he'd said to her the day before they packed up and headed for the Mazatzals.

"Do not worry so, *mi hija*, for I'll be careful, and I won't let you and your brother be hurt. But this is our chance to be rich. I'll finally be able to give you and Miguel all of the things that I was never able to give your mother."

Alicia had given up then, for she knew it was useless. What he was doing wasn't so much for them, as it was for the woman he believed he'd failed. Maybe all that had happened to them had been inevitable.

The bandit called Farley stirred from his place in the corner. She turned to see what he was up to.

"You there, girl, bring me one of them canteens," he ordered.

Alicia struggled to keep her anger under control and her tongue in check. Without a word to him, she turned her attention to what lay outside the doorway. Decker ignored him too. When Farley saw that she wasn't jumping to accommodate him, he got up and headed for the water containers.

Decker was standing at the far end of the pallet, holding a Winchester. He brought the barrel up ever so slightly, and aimed it directly at Farley's leg. The outlaw saw it and froze where he stood.

"Can't a fellow have a drink once in awhile?" he whined.

Alicia noted how quickly his voice had lost its arrogance. The man disgusted her.

"Get back to your place," Decker ordered. "You've already had your share, and then some."

Farley kept his gaze riveted on the barrel of the rifle as he slunk back to the corner. Alicia was glad that Decker was with them. Miguel had gone outside earlier to keep watch for outlaws and Apaches. She glanced at the gold that had been stacked against the wall. Those burlap bags made the house seem even smaller. How she wished that her father could have found a fraction of that amount of gold. It would have made all the difference in their lives. First off, they could have left the mountains before the Apaches killed him. Then he could have bought them a nice house, something that her mother had always wanted, and something that she wanted, too. During the years since her mother had died of the wasting disease, they'd become wanderers. She knew that her father had been looking for peace and that he'd been unable to find it. One thing, for sure: Alicia was sick of wandering.

The wounded man moaned and pushed away his coverings. He was no longer chilling. She went over and felt his forehead. He was flushed and running a fever.

"Can I do anything?" Decker asked.

"Not unless you know some prayers."

"I'll give it a try, but I intend to pray with my eyes open."

"Around here that's the only way."

She took Jake's bandana and poured water on it from the canteen.

"Hey!" yelled Farley. "Stop that!"

Alicia ignored him.

"Decker, did you see that? She's wasting water when I can't even wet my whistle."

"Shut up," Decker ordered.

Alicia bathed the sick man's face, trying to cool it down a little. His chest was bare, for his shirt had been stripped off in order to deal with his wound. She washed his chest with the wet cloth, hoping it would make a difference.

As she sat beside him, he tossed and turned, occasionally muttering something unintelligible. Outside, it was growing darker. This was the time they should be moving out, but they couldn't move Jake, not just yet.

"We're going to have to stay," Decker said, as if reading her thoughts.

"I know."

Miguel appeared in the doorway.

"There's no sign of anyone, at least not yet," he said. "I'm hungry. Is there anything left to eat?"

"There's piñon nuts and jerky in one of the saddlebags," said Decker. "And some dried apples too."

"Gi'me some of that," Farley ordered.

Miguel searched the saddle bags, ignoring the outlaw. When he found what he was looking for, they shared a meager meal, all except Jake.

Afterward, Decker held the gun while Miguel tied the outlaw securely.

"We'll take turns keeping watch," Decker said.

"Are you sure you trust me?" Miguel asked.

"When your interests and mine are the same, I'd trust you with my life. Besides, I've got no choice. I'll take the first watch."

"I will do it," Alicia said. "You're tired."

"Thanks. But you need to look after my partner. You're better at that than I am. If you need any help call me."

Decker went outside and Miguel spread his bedroll in the doorway.

Alicia liked Decker. She judged him to be her own age, or very close to it. But he'd had an easy life, that much was clear. He was what her father would have called a spoiled young man of means. She wondered what he was doing teamed up with Jake Lockridge, who was clearly not a spoiled young man of means. At least he hadn't been a man of means until now, and his future depended on what happened tonight and during the next few days.

After she'd done all she could for her patient, Alicia stepped over Miguel's sleeping form and went outside. Farley had been snoring for some time, and she was reasonably certain that he wasn't feigning sleep. She stood near the house for a few minutes, trying to make out Decker's outline in the darkness. He must have noticed her, for he called out.

"Over here."

She walked over to where he was standing beside a creosote bush.

"How is he?"

"The same," she said. "I'm hoping the fever will break soon."

"Good, for we can't stay here long."

Alicia agreed. They were taking a big risk by spending the night.

"Do you think we got by without the Apaches noticing us?"

"Probably," he said. "I think that if they knew we were here, they'd have attacked before dark."

"What about the outlaws?"

"Culebra lost a man and another one is wounded. That accounts for half of them, although I expect there are others elsewhere. His gang is reputed to be much larger than what we've seen. Culebra likes the deck stacked in his favor, and this time it isn't. He may settle for trailing us and trying to pick us off from a distance."

Alicia shivered and it wasn't from the cold that was descending on the desert.

"I guess you'll be glad to get back to your folks," Decker said, changing the subject.

"They're not my folks. They were friends of my mother from long ago. I don't know them at all, and I feel like a beggar going to them and asking for shelter. If it were only for myself, I wouldn't do it. But Papa told us that if anything happened to him that was where we were to go."

These past days, she'd been thinking a lot about their plight. The more she thought about begging for a home, the more she hated it. Work was scarce for a woman, though, and Miguel was barely sixteen. Still, anything would be better than what faced them in Hermosillo.

She pulled her *mantón* securely around her shoulders, for a wind from the north was causing a chill.

Alicia thought of her father and his years of tragedy. She felt sad because he'd lost control of his life so long ago. Maybe no one ever ruled their own lives, although it didn't seem that way to her. Some appeared to have things exactly the way they wanted them. She looked up at the pinpoints of light in the Arizona sky and made a wish. It was the same wish that she always made—the power to direct her own life.

Decker had been respecting her silence. But it had lengthened.

"Are you okay, Ma'am?" he asked.

"Yes. And please call me Alicia. I believe we're friends now."

Decker chuckled.

"What's funny?" she asked.

"When we met over on the Verde, I wouldn't have bet a piece of moldy hardtack that we'd ever come close to being friends."

She remembered it that way as well. For so long, everyone had been their enemy, and the two *gringos* had looked dangerous. It was Miguel who'd insisted that the best defense is an attack. So, instead of hiding until the strangers had left, they'd attacked. The gold had astonished her. She still wasn't sure she believed it, and it was stacked against the wall of the old house. She could look any time she chose.

"Life is strange," she answered. "I hope we all get out of this alive."

Decker acted like he was mulling something over. Then he spoke.

"Look, you and your brother had some hard luck that you didn't deserve. Then you helped us fight off the outlaws, and you helped Jake when he needed that bullet pulled out. Now, I'm not an equal partner with Jake. I'm only in on this for a fifth of what we've taken out. But I want to share that fifth with you and Miguel on a fifty-fifty basis. You deserve it."

Alicia was surprised and touched by his offer. According to her figures, that would be a tenth of the treasure. A tithe. That was more than she'd dreamed of, and it would be enough to get her and Miguel started on a better life somewhere. Decker was right about them sharing danger, and she had tended Jake's wound as best she could. This offer of gold wasn't charity that would shame her.

"Thank you," she said. "That amount of gold would mean a great deal to us. We would no longer need to go begging to former friends, and that would please my mother very much if she's in a position to know."

"Good, then it's settled."

There was something else on her mind.

"What do you know about this Culebra?" she asked. "Is he from Mexico?"

"Actually, I don't know a whole lot. I heard them talking about him in Prescott, though. They say that Culebra is Irish. A fellow who seemed to know what he was talking about said that his real name was Fitzgerald, or something like that."

"Odd. I wonder why they call him the Spanish word for snake."

"Maybe because he's mean and dangerous, and he strikes when you're not expecting it. They say he's killed a lot of men, and that's on top of rustling and robbing."

"I guess the name fits."

"Better get some rest," Decker advised. "Who knows what tomorrow will bring."

During the night, she heard Miguel get up and go to relieve Decker at his post. Then she heard Decker spread out his bedroll and crawl into it. Jake was breathing strong and steady. He was no longer tossing and turning, nor was he muttering in his sleep. This was a good sign. She crawled over and felt his forehead. The fever had broken.

When she awoke at dawn, she was surprised to find Jake standing over her. Startled, she scrambled to her feet.

"Sorry," he apologized. "I didn't mean to frighten you. It's just that we need to pull out of here right away. We've stayed too long already."

"Of course," she said. "It won't take much time to pack up."

He gave her a searching look.

"Some of the things that happened, I remember, and some of them I don't. But I know I owe you a lot. Thanks."

"*Da nada*," she replied. "It was nothing."

Jake turned then and started loading the pack animals as best he could with one arm. Decker and Miguel came to his assistance. Farley sat in the corner and complained until they were ready to leave.

"Are you going to make me walk some more?" Farley asked.

"We have no choice," Jake said. "It's either you walk or I shoot you."

It seemed to her that Jake was his old self again. Except that he held his left arm close to his side, he looked the same.

She wondered if Decker would keep his rash promise to share the gold with them. If he did, it would make a world of difference. If not, she would find a way to survive without going begging. This would be the first step in shaping her life instead of surrendering to the forces around her. But if the man they called "Snake" caught up with them, nothing would really matter anyway.

Chapter Ten

It wasn't long before they were packed and ready to leave the adobe house that had sheltered them. Jake felt a dull pain where he'd been wounded and he still felt weak. But he could ride. He had to ride. His instincts were telling him that trouble was coming.

The gold was safely packed on the mules and the horse that they'd found wandering alone. He was grateful to Alicia Sandoval for her help and he wanted to share some of the treasure with her and her brother. But he didn't know how to talk to her about it. She was so proud and sensitive. Miguel was even worse. *There's time to talk about it later. Right now, we have to survive.*

"Let's ride," he said.

They moved out, riding in silence except for Farley's grumbling. But the footsore outlaw managed to keep pace.

Overhead, the sky was growing lighter. Not a single cloud graced the blue canopy above them. Stretching before them were miles of arid land that was filled with cactuses, stately yuccas, spindly ocotillo plants, and other vegetation that could survive on limited rainfall. As time passed, the sun rose higher and grew hotter. Jake began looking for a place where they could stop until evening. Their shelter needed to have shade but, above all, it had to be defensible. It was almost midday when they entered a narrow canyon with steep sides. The canyon was dotted with *saguero*, and it contained creosote bushes and paloverde trees. Here and there, clumps of yuccas showed their spiky leaves. He decided that the canyon would do. Farley, who was staggering along at the end of his endurance had stopped complaining. It was costing him too much effort.

"This is good enough," Jake said. "We'll make camp here until nightfall."

The announcement was met with expressions of relief.

"It's about time," Farley said. "I've just about had it with this forced march you've got me on, and don't go threatening to shoot me. Right about now, I just plain don't care."

While the outlaw threw himself down to rest, Miguel and Decker unloaded the animals. Then Decker helped Alicia gather fuel for a campfire. Jake kept an eye on Farley, while at the same time he was on the lookout for unwelcome company.

Decker helped Alicia to build a small fire that wouldn't be noticeable at a distance. When this was done, she put the coffee pot on to boil. Jake was glad that Nate had packed a good supply of coffee, for there were times when the hot brew could change a man's entire outlook.

Decker was rationing the food at Jake's suggestion, so no single one of them got very much. Still, with something in his stomach and a cup of hot coffee in his hand, Jake felt almost human again. His only complaint would have been the pain in his shoulder.

He thought about the days since he'd left Phoenix and taken on a partner. It seemed to him that Decker's appearance had changed since he'd found him stranded in the desert. Muscles had replaced flab. He walked straighter, too, which added to his height. Not only that, his beard had grown, giving him a mature look. He'd left off whining and complaining. What's more, he saw what needed to be done and he did it. Jake wondered what Grandfather Kemp would think of his runaway grandson if he could see him. He doubted if the old man would have the nerve to try forcing Decker into the law profession now, considering his newly acquired confidence and strength.

Alicia took the pot and refilled his cup. Decker and Miguel had finished eating and were sprawled on their bedrolls for some much needed sleep.

"When this danger is over, are you going to stay in Arizona?" she asked.

Jake wasn't sure how to answer her question. Since Nate's death, he hadn't thought much past getting the gold to a safe place and avenging his uncle's murder. Maybe it was still too early for him to be making plans, but Alicia had started him to thinking. After the gang had been dealt with, he was going to have to make a life for himself.

"Maybe I'll stay in Arizona," he said. "Right now, I just don't know."

"There was a woman in California," she announced as if she knew it for a fact. "I think she must have been very beautiful."

"Why do you think that?"

She gazed off into the distance.

"A woman has a way of knowing these things," she said enigmatically.

Jake figured that he must have talked about Helen while he was fighting that fever.

"There was, as a matter of fact," he admitted. "But she was a smart lady. She married a fellow with a lot better prospects than a run-down cowpoke was likely to have."

"Then she was a fool."

Her remark startled him.

"I appreciate your kind words," he managed to say.

"A modest man sometimes needs a big dose of the truth," she replied.

It seemed to Jake that he'd been changing his opinions a lot of late. He'd changed his opinion of Decker and now he was changing his opinion of the Sandovals. It was a fact that Miguel had taken on responsibility when he was needed and Alicia had tended his wound. Still, he felt the need for caution. Trust didn't come easy for him.

The long walk had tired Farley out and he was blessedly asleep. Alicia went about finishing her chores. Then she went over to lie down near her brother. With Decker asleep, Jake was left alone to keep vigil.

No sound or sight disturbed him. All was as it should be, and he was struggling to stay awake by the time Decker woke up to take his turn. Grateful for the chance to get some rest, himself, Jake spread out a blanket. At dusk, he opened his eyes feeling better than he'd felt since he'd been shot. Alicia glanced over and saw that he was awake. Quickly she got up and handed him a cup of some kind of hot liquid.

"Drink it," she ordered. "It will give you strength."

He sniffed it first, and then tasted it cautiously. It turned out that she'd concocted a soup from bits of dried beef, piñon nuts, and other ingredients that were a mystery. The soup was easy to swallow, and he was hungry. It looked as if the others had already eaten.

"It's good," he said. "Thanks."

"Hunger is a good sign," she said with approval. "You're a strong man and I expect your wound will heal quickly."

"I expect it will," he agreed as he handed her the cup for a refill.

Jake noticed that Farley was sitting nearby, watching with heavy-lidded eyes. He wondered what the outlaw was plotting.

Before he could finish the soup, Farley spoke up.

"Hey, Lockridge, you mentioned that you were headed for Phoenix, didn't you?"

Immediately, Jake was on his guard.

"I may have mentioned it. What of it?"

"I reckon you'll be dropping me off at the jail, then."

Jake was suspicious.

"No, I wasn't planning on it."

It was plain that Farley didn't like his answer.

"How come? It's what anybody else would do."

Jake handed the empty cup to Alicia who was listening with interest. He'd caught the attention of Decker and Miguel as well.

"Maybe, but I doubt if Phoenix is a safe place for me, right now, or for my gold," he replied.

"But I thought you were going to take me and my brother there," Alicia said.

"Not quite. I'm taking you close to Phoenix. You'll have to go the rest of the way on your own."

"I see," she said. "Well, that is better than nothing, I guess."

Jake turned to Decker. "We need to get a horse for Farley and a couple of spares for ourselves, not to mention some supplies. It'd be a good idea if you rode into town with the Sandovals. See what you can find. I'll stay a safe distance away with Farley and the pack animals."

That seemed to mitigate, if only slightly, Farley's disappointment in not being headed for the Phoenix jail. It made Jake wonder how long it would have taken him to break free of that little hoosegow and rejoin the gang.

"It's about time you got me a horse," the outlaw complained. "I've done enough walking to last me from now on."

"At least you're alive and able to do it," Decker reminded him.

The thought didn't seem to bring much satisfaction to him as he rubbed his feet.

Jake turned to Alicia.

"It won't be long now, before you and your brother are safe in Mexico at the home of your friends."

She didn't look encouraged, and he wished he hadn't mentioned it.

When it was fully dark, they saddled up and headed out. At the far end of the canyon, the walls gradually receded, until they flattened entirely. Jake and the others were ushered into a large valley.

He noticed that Alicia was keeping her distance, and he figured she needed time for her own thoughts. He understood the need for privacy because he was that way himself. But after a time, Miguel rode up beside him.

"My sister is a little upset, but I guess you've noticed."

"Oh? What's she upset about?"

"It's those friends in Mexico. We scarcely know them, and Alicia dreads going there and imposing on them. She thinks we ought to make our own way in the world."

"What do you think?" Jake asked.

"I agree. But I think she worries that she won't be able to do that. She worries about her responsibility to me. But I can work too. That is, if I get a chance."

Miguel was making Jake feel like some kind of godfather who was failing in his duty. He didn't much like it.

"I expect you'll get a chance to work, or else you'll make one," he told the boy. "Possibly you can find work in Phoenix."

"I'm going to try."

They rode side by side for a time without talking until Farley started harassing them.

"Ain't none of you going to have to worry about making a living, 'cause ain't none of you going to live. If them Apaches don't get you first, Culebra is sure to catch you. He's not about to let you get away after what you've done to him."

Jake figured he hadn't done anything but defend himself and his property.

"Shut your mouth, Farley," he said. "Whatever happens to us, you're going to be right smack in the middle of it. You're just as apt to catch a bullet as anyone else."

The thought appeared to sober the outlaw a little.

"Well, if you want to outdistance them, you'd better make that half-growed kid get off his horse and let me ride it for awhile," he said. "I ain't as young and spry as I used to be."

Jake reined up and glared at Farley.

"I'm not about to make a man give up his horse to a no-account who tried to kill me. If you can't keep up with us, I'll be glad to leave you out here for buzzard bait. It's not quite the same as hanging, but it'll serve the same purpose."

Miguel was infuriated by what Farley had said.

"Any coyote who tries to take my horse and put me afoot isn't going to have need of a horse anymore," he promised, looking down on the outlaw from his place in the saddle.

Farley knew when he'd gone too far. He backed down and shut his mouth.

They traveled throughout the night, stopping often to rest, for Farley demanded it. Come daybreak, they stopped to rest beneath a hump-back mountain. Jake knew they were close to Phoenix.

He ground-staked the animals while Farley sat down and pulled his boots off.

"I've got blisters on blisters," he complained.

"Why don't you tell it to somebody who cares," said Miguel as he glared at the outlaw with disgust.

They'd come a long way, but Jake felt sad. This

was a time of parting. Alicia and her brother were going to Phoenix while he was going west. It helped him some to know that Decker would be escorting them into town. After they'd rested awhile, he said what was difficult for him to say.

"The three of you had best mount up and be on your way. It'll be getting hotter before long."

He took some gold pieces from a small pouch that he carried in one of his saddlebags and handed them to Decker.

"Get the best horses you can with that," he said.

Then he turned to Alicia who stood beside her mare, looking a little bit lost.

"Thank you for your help, *Señorita*. Your brother has been helpful too."

"*Da nada*," she said. "What we did was nothing."

Awkwardly, he placed several gold pieces into her hands.

"You've both earned this, and maybe it will help you to get a new start."

"Just a minute," Decker interrupted. "I forgot to tell you that I promised Alicia and Miguel half of my fifth."

"Well, you can't give it to them, now," Jake said. "Toting even a tenth of what we have into Phoenix would be suicide, especially since Farley has friends there."

"How do you know that?"

"From the things that he's said, and from the way he's been acting."

They all looked at Farley, who cursed in spite of the fact that Alicia was standing nearby. Jake noticed that she simply gazed off into the distance as if the likes of Farley didn't exist. To him, she looked like the elegant daughter of a Spanish Don.

"Trust me," Decker said to the Sandovals. "After the gold is safe, I'll come back to Phoenix and find you."

Miguel looked skeptical at the *gringo's* promise and Alicia seemed to take no notice at all of what he'd just said. The gold pieces she'd been given had disappeared somewhere in the folds of her skirt.

She climbed on the mare and got ready to ride. She was as beautiful as ever. Decker and Miguel mounted up too.

"I guess this is good-bye," she said, looking sadly at Jake.

"I guess so," he agreed, feeling awkward. "Take care of yourself now."

As they rode away, he stood watching them for a long time.

"Now ain't that touching," Farley taunted.

Jake had his fill. He balled his hands into fists and stood in front of the outlaw.

"If you've got anything more to say on the subject, you're going to find yourself walking every step of the way to Arizona City—after I've given you a licking with my good arm."

The threat worked. Farley kept his mouth shut for a good long time after that.

Now, if Culebra didn't find him before Decker got back, and if Farley's friends in Phoenix didn't show up, Jake figured that he might just have a fighting chance.

Chapter Eleven

It was late afternoon when Decker returned from town. He was leading a pretty mare with a blaze, a roan, and a large bay. From a distance, it looked like he'd made some good choices.

"Have any trouble?" he asked when Decker rode up.

"Nope. In fact it was kind of fun. I believe I may have a natural talent for horse trading."

"How about Alicia and her brother? Are they all right?"

"Yes, they're fine. I hung around for awhile just to make sure. Alicia got a job cooking at the cafe, and the owner is letting her sleep on a cot in the back. Miguel is working at the livery stable down the street. The old man who runs the place told him he could stay there at night."

"That's good to know," Jake said, relieved that they were safe, at least. Somewhere along the way, he'd grown to feel responsible for them. But deep down, he wanted something better for Alicia than cooking in a sweltering kitchen and sleeping on a backroom cot. He wanted something better for Miguel too. Maybe after this business was settled, he could return with Decker and see to it that they got a better deal.

"Oh, I almost forgot," said Decker. "I brought you a present."

He reached into one of his saddlebags and pulled out a pie.

"Where did you come up with this?"

"A widow woman in Phoenix bakes 'em. They're supposed to be good, and I thought it was worth taking a chance on."

Jake took his knife and cut the dried apple pie into thirds. He handed one to Decker and one to Farley, not that he thought Farley merited a third of his pie. Then he proceeded to eat his own share with considerable pleasure. He allowed that Decker was as good at picking out pies as he was at picking horses.

Because he'd stayed awake throughout most of the day guarding Farley, and because he'd ridden all night the night before, Jake was bone tired. After he'd eaten, he put Decker in charge and fell asleep. When Decker shook him awake, the stars were already out. Everything had been loaded, and they were ready to get underway.

"You must be hurting for sleep by now yourself," Jake said.

"I'll be okay. Don't worry about me."

Jake wondered, again, where the spoiled greenhorn had gone that he'd found in the desert such a short time before. Decker had changed.

Jake, Decker, and their prisoner headed toward the southwest, leaving the solitary mountain behind them. With Farley mounted on the mare, they were able to make good time. Jake should have felt pleased about that, but he had the nagging feeling that he was leaving behind some unfinished business.

Now that he was riding instead of walking, Farley's complaints had stopped. His other comments had stopped as well. The outlaw acted as if he expected something to happen, and this troubled Jake. Not only was Culebra and the two surviving outlaws following them, but Jake suspected that they'd soon be joined by the other members of the gang who were certain to be hiding out somewhere around Phoenix.

He was also aware that now Farley was astride a fast horse, he was more likely to try to escape. Jake decided to worry him a little.

"You know, Farley, if you make a break for it, I'm going to have to shoot you."

"Yeah. You'd probably do it too."

"Then make sure you don't give me an excuse."

Jake glanced over at Decker. After a night and day without rest, the kid appeared to be asleep in the saddle. It was left up to him to guard the outlaw and to stay alert.

The night was clear. The stars were bright over the Sonoran Desert and they appeared to be close to the Earth. He needed to figure out what he was going to do with his life once the treasure was secure. He could go back to California, of course, but that seemed like another world to him now. Maybe he would stay on in Arizona. Nate had loved it so well. After all, he knew something about the cattle business, and ranches had sprung up over the Territory despite the risks involved.

"You think you're in the clear now, don't you, Lockridge?" Farley taunted after a long stint of keeping his mouth shut.

The new confidence in his voice disturbed Jake.

"Is there any reason why I shouldn't?" he asked.

The outlaw's laugh was derisive.

"You think you're pretty smart because you caught on about some of the boys being in town," he said. "But Culebra, Nettles, and McQuay are going to trail you back to Phoenix and hook up with 'em. Then the whole bunch is going to come after you. You and that kid don't stand a chance, and that's a fact."

Farley was gloating.

"Then they'll just have to come after us and see what kind of reception they get."

"The odds ain't too good, at least not for you. It'll be six against two. Seven counting myself."

Jake had to agree with him. The odds were miserable. But at least he knew what to expect now, and he had the satisfaction of knowing that Alicia and Miguel were safe in Phoenix. He decided to give Farley something to think about.

"Maybe you're the one who ought to start worrying. You're apt to face a hangman's noose once we get to Arizona City."

"I'm not worried. You ain't got the chance of a slab of gingerbread at a Sunday School picnic of gettin' me there."

"I guess we'll just have to find out about that."

A couple of hours before daylight, they came to a dip in the landscape. It was actually a shallow bowl where they would be out of sight of anyone who was following. It was here that Jake decided to make camp.

"Get down," he ordered Farley.

Efficiently, he bound the outlaw's wrists and ankles, while Farley protested the treatment in strong terms.

Decker managed to put a fresh bandage on his wound before Jake insisted that the kid get some sleep.

"I'll take the first watch," he said. "You need to be ready for whatever is coming."

Decker didn't argue. He spread out his bedroll and was soon snoring.

"You'd better cook up a big breakfast," said Farley. "We're apt to have company come daylight."

Jake ignored the remark, but he knew the outlaw could be right. When it started to get light, he made his way to the rim and looked over the top. It was possible to see for a long way and no riders were visible. Even though they were sure to be outnumbered, at least they wouldn't be surprised. It looked like Farley was wrong about having company for breakfast. Supper, however, was another matter.

As the day progressed, it became a scorcher. Farley crawled under the shade of a creosote bush and went to sleep. Jake unbuttoned his shirt, but it didn't help much. Already, he was missing the coolness of the mountains in spite of the dangers there. He longed for a drink of water from a cold mountain spring.

He worried about Alicia and how she'd be working in an oven-hot kitchen just to survive. But at least she was safe there. He resolved, once and for all, that he'd go back to Phoenix with Decker and share the gold with them. But now, all he could do was wait and watch.

Eventually Farley woke up, and with his hands still bound, he started fanning himself with his hat. There was no breeze in the natural "bowl" that they were camped in. This made it more uncomfortable than it would have been up on the flat.

"Are you planning on pulling up stakes come dark?" Farley asked.

"Don't I always?"

"Can't rightly say. I ain't knowed you that long."

"Then you'll just have to wait and find out."

"Well, if you've got it in mind to stay ahead of the boss, you'd better haul yourself out of here right now."

It was clear what he was trying to do. He was trying to force Jake to abandon their hiding place so they'd be visible to the outlaws if they were anywhere close. Not only that, the heat would take its toll on them.

Jake got up and stretched all six feet of himself until he towered over the reclining outlaw.

"I've been real patient with you, Farley, but if you're smart, you'll not be pressing your luck from here on out."

Whatever else the outlaw had been going to say, he kept to himself.

Jake walked around the perimeter of the campsite, as much to keep awake as to exercise his legs. He knew that if he dozed off in the heat that Farley would try to escape. Truth to tell, he wouldn't mind all that much being rid of him, but the outlaw would try to steal the horses and the gold, and most likely, he'd shoot his captors.

He'd made a dozen rounds when Decker woke up and offered to take his place.

"Get some rest, Lockridge. I'll make sure that Farley behaves himself."

Jake was glad to turn it over to him.

"Just make sure to check over the rim once in awhile, but keep your head down. If they're out there, you don't want them to spot you."

"I'll take care of it," he promised.

Jake spread out his blanket and sprawled on it. Soon he was asleep. He wasn't sure how much time had passed when he was awakened by a loud commotion. Tin bounced off stone, followed by a loud yelp. He grabbed for his revolver and sprang to his feet. Farley was astride the mare, going over the top of the basin. By the time Jake got a bead on him, it was too late.

He turned back to see Decker hopping around on one foot. The kid was swearing that he was going to kill Farley just as soon as he could get his hands on him.

"What happened?" Jake asked.

Decker settled down then. He had a look of pain and embarrassment on his face.

"That no-good coyote got away. Stole a horse too."

"How did it happen?"

"Guess I got a little careless. I was taking the coffeepot off the fire when he slipped up behind me and struck me. I dropped the pot and scalded myself with coffee."

Decker should never have turned his back on the outlaw, but he knew that now. There wasn't any point in Jake giving him a lecture.

"It's over," he said. "Just be more careful next time. If you want to know the truth about it, I'm glad that he's gone. He was gettin' on my nerves."

Decker dropped his pants and placed a wet rag on his scalded thigh.

"I guess it could have been worse," he said. "He could have busted my skull open."

Jake figured he was right about that. Any humanity that Farley may have once had was long gone.

"I guess we're not going to go after the mare then, *amigo*?"

"Nope," said Jake. "We're going to haul this gold

to Arizona City. That's our priority. I'm beginning to think it was worth the mare to get rid of that loud mouth."

Jake didn't tell him that he hated like poison to lose that little mare. Decker had a good eye for horse flesh, no question about it. Besides, the mare belonged to him, and he liked to keep what was his.

As soon as the sun dipped below the horizon, they got ready to move out. At dark, they topped the rim. He figured that Farley had backtracked to find Culebra, in spite of the fact that the leader had abandoned him. Farley wanted the gold and he needed help to steal it, even though that meant splitting it with the others.

"Shouldn't we be getting close to the Gila River?" Decker asked after they'd been in the saddle for a time.

"We should be, at least to the best of my recollection."

"Well, I'd feel a whole lot easier if we could be across that river before the outlaws catch sight of us."

Jake wasn't sure why, for it wasn't all that much of a barrier. But beyond the river was the mountains, and if they had to make a stand, the mountains was the place to do it.

"Do you think that we did the right thing, not bringing the Sandovals with us?" Decker asked.

"No doubt about it. At least they're safe where they are. You may soon be wishing you were back there with them, or back in Prescott."

"It's strange," Decker said. "I thought that getting the gold out of the Mazatzals would be the hardest part, but I was wrong."

"*Amigo*, there's not any easy parts. But if we can pull this off, it'll give us both a good start, and the Sandovals too."

All the while they were riding in the darkness, Jake was alert for both Apaches and outlaws. Decker appeared to be lost in thought. After a time, he spoke up.

"If Culebra really is on our trail, then Farley shouldn't have any trouble finding him and bringing him and his outfit straight to us."

"That's about the way I've got it sized up."

It was enough to make a man give up on his future. But he'd never forgotten something that Nate had told him when he was just a kid.

"Son, sometimes a man gets into a predicament where he doesn't have any chance at all," he'd said. "That's when he's got to get busy and make himself one."

That was a whole lot easier said than done. But that was exactly what he was going to have to do—make himself a chance.

But first off, he was going to get across the Gila River. He began pushing the horses and the mules for greater speed. When they got closer the animals could smell the water, and the promise of a drink urged them on.

The animals slaked their thirst and he and Decker

filled their canteens. Then they crossed the river in moonlight. The dark shadows that loomed ahead were the Gila Bend Mountains. They were still a long way from their destination, but they were closer than before. Jake looked skyward to the stars that made up the Big Dipper. They seemed distant and removed from human difficulties. Yet, those same stars were over California, and they were also over Phoenix. In a mysterious way the thought was comforting, but not for long.

"I sure hope that none of those sidewinders run into Alicia and Miguel back in town," Decker thought aloud.

The kid couldn't seem to keep his mind off of Phoenix.

"The ones in town wouldn't recognize them," he said.

"But what if Culebra or one of his outfit saw her during the shoot-out, and what if Farley goes back there?"

Jake didn't want to think about that.

"Alicia and Miguel don't have what Culebra wants. They don't even know where we are. We're the ones the outlaws are after."

"I guess you're saying that I ought to keep worrying about my own hide."

"If worrying ever does any good."

The truth was, Jake was worrying enough for both of them.

Chapter Twelve

Much to Alicia's relief, the stifling hot day was finally over. Although she'd gone to work soon after her arrival, this had been her first full day on the job. The cafe was closed and she was enjoying the privacy of the back room. She dipped a cloth into a bowl of water and washed her face and shoulders. The excess dribbled downward, cooling more of her body. For hours, the kitchen had been a kind of purgatory. Now, she actually thought she might survive. With a deft motion, she pulled her blouse back into place. After wringing out the cloth, she went to the back door and stepped outside. A breeze from the south touched the wetness of her skin, causing her to shiver with pleasure.

The gold coins that Jake had given her might keep them for a time, but when they were spent, it would leave her and Miguel penniless. She wondered if Decker would keep his word about coming back and giving them half of his share. She had no doubt that when he made the promise he was sincere, but promises were easily forgotten.

Alicia permitted herself a few moments of refreshment before returning to her room. She almost forgot about the loose board that was nailed across the bottom of the doorway and nearly stumbled on it. Dodson, who owned the cafe, wasn't good about keeping up on repairs. Alicia would have complained, but since it was her first full day she decided it would be wiser to wait awhile. She left the door open, letting the night breezes cool the stuffy room.

There was only a strip of moonlight to illuminate her surroundings. Using a small kitchen knife, she made a brief slit in the mattress. Then quickly she retrieved the cloth-wrapped gold pieces from a pocket in her skirt and stuffed them inside the opening. It was the best she could do for a hiding place, at least for the time being.

Next, she placed a poker within reach. This was just in case a drunken cowhand or a wild animal wandered in. Then she gently eased her tired body onto the cot. With a sigh, she closed her eyes.

Tomorrow would bring another hot day of labor in the kitchen. She thought of Miguel who would be asleep by now. The hay at the livery stable would make a soft bed and, no doubt, he was as tired from his workday as she. Alicia promised herself that she would rise early enough to see him for a few minutes before beginning her duties. Things would get better for them, she promised. She would just have to make sure that they did. Soon she fell into an exhausted sleep.

A noise awakened her suddenly in the night. Someone had tripped on the board across the doorway. She kept her eyes shut as she eased her hand downward and grasped the poker. She could smell the unwashed body of a man inside her room. His breathing was heavy and irregular. Suddenly a beefy hand covered her mouth. She brought the poker up sharply, jabbing it into a fatty paunch of stomach. He staggered backward with a curse. Alicia scrambled from the cot, her weapon poised to strike again.

Her assailant grabbed at the poker and yanked it from her hand. She heard it rattle as it hit the floor. Before she could squirm away from him, he had her by the hair, forcing her to him. She felt the sharp edge of a knife blade against the skin of her throat.

"If you want to live, woman, you'll keep your mouth shut and do as I tell you."

The order was delivered in a raspy whisper.

"I've got your brother outside."

Alicia's fear turned to panic. She had no doubt this was one of Culebra's outlaws, and he'd kidnapped Miguel.

Clutching her tightly by her hair and keeping the knife at her throat, the outlaw walked her down the alley to where the horses were waiting. She saw that one of them was her own mare. But draped over another horse was Miguel. She couldn't tell whether he was unconscious or dead.

"What have you done to him?" she demanded to know.

"Don't worry. He's just taking a little nap. He'll be coming around soon, that is if you behave yourself."

Believing the threat would be sufficient to ensure her cooperation, he eased the knife away from her throat.

"Now, get on that horse and do as you're told. If you let out a peep, I swear I'll put a bullet into your brother's head."

Fear and hatred seethed within her as she climbed into the saddle. Sitting astride, she let her wide skirts fall to either side. The outlaw kept his mount a little behind so he could keep a close watch on her.

"Let's go," he ordered as he prepared to follow her and lead Miguel's horse.

The town was dark and deathly quiet as they headed west.

She guessed that he was taking them to the rest of the gang. Culebra must have linked them to the gold. Was he wanting to make a trade, perhaps? Was the life of Alicia Sandoval worth the treasure of the Mazatzals?

When the town was far behind them and she believed it would be safe to speak, she asked where they were being taken.

"Shut up!" was her answer.

She felt like a trapped animal. Escape was out of

the question, though, for there was Miguel to consider. It would be unthinkable to leave her brother behind with such a man. Every time she looked over and saw him trussed up like a bag of grain, she was sick with anger. She resolved that, somehow, she was going to make the outlaw pay for what he'd done to them.

At last, she heard her brother moan, as if he were coming around. When he lost the contents of his stomach, the outlaw stopped.

"Take care of him," he ordered. "But make it quick. I don't intend to hang around here for long."

Alicia dismounted and pulled Miguel from the horse. He was heavy. As gently as possible, she eased him to the ground.

"What happened?" he asked as he struggled to bring her face into focus in the pre-dawn light.

"You were struck on the head and kidnapped. Then I was taken too."

She lightly touched the bruise on the side of his forehead and saw him wince. With the bandana that she pulled from his neck, Alicia cleaned him up as best she could.

"He needs water," she informed the outlaw.

Grudgingly, he handed her a canteen.

"Better not give him much, for it's got to last."

Miguel managed a few swallows before he was commanded to stop.

"Enough!" said the outlaw as he snatched the canteen away from Miguel's grasp and strode back to his horse.

"Where are we?" Miguel whispered.

"West of town, but not far. He's taking us to the rest of the gang."

"That's enough whispering, you two," the outlaw interrupted. "Climb on those horses and get ready to ride."

Alicia could tell that Miguel was still disoriented due to the blow he'd sustained. She helped him to his horse and waited for him to mount. Then she went over to the mare. When they rode on at the outlaw's command, she was relieved that her brother was able to stay in the saddle. Still, that had been a hard blow and she worried about him. She was worried about both of them.

Once they caught up with the rest of the gang, she knew there would be little chance of escape. They would have to make their move while there was only one guard to worry about. Miguel's hands were tied, so it would be up to her. But while her hands were free, she was weaponless. Somehow, she would have to find one.

It seemed like an eternity before their captor stopped again. It was fully daylight and the darkness that would have been her ally was gone. The horses rested while the outlaw built himself a smoke. All the while, he kept watch on the prisoners. Alicia found a place to sit on the ground near her brother. His hands were tied in front, in view of the outlaw, so there was nothing she could do about his bonds. She put her own hand on the ground beside her and felt around for a rock. There was none within reach that was suitable for a weapon. She checked to see that the outlaw was enjoying his cigarette. Then careful not to attract attention, she scooted over a few feet. Again, she reached out, searching. This time her fingers closed over a rock that was small enough to conceal in her hand, yet large enough to do some damage if used in the right way. She slid it beneath the folds of her skirt and slipped it into a side pocket.

When the outlaw finished smoking, he tossed the remains away, yawned, and stretched his arms. It was clear that he thought they were helpless for he'd let his guard down. Now that his hand was far away from his holster, she had a chance. She grasped the rock and hurled it at him with all of her strength. The missile caught him right between the eyes. He crumpled like a rag doll. Alicia ran over and disarmed him. Then using the knife that he'd held at her throat, she went and freed Miguel.

"We've got to get out of here," she said.

"Are you going to leave him any water?"

Alicia thought of the treatment they'd received at the outlaw's hands and almost refused. Then she relented.

"We'll leave him only a little," she replied. "He's not all that far from Phoenix and it'll do him good to walk."

She grabbed hold of the horses' reins while Miguel rubbed the circulation back into his wrists.

"Does this mean we're not going back to town?" he asked.

"Not directly. We're going to have to find Jake and Decker and warn them."

"But they're west of here. The rest of the outlaws must be too. If we keep on like this, we're sure to run into Culebra and his men."

She was aware of the danger but she hoped to avoid the outlaws and reach Jake before they did.

"Hurry up!" she ordered. "I've no intention of running into him. I'm not blind, you know."

He gave her a look that she was accustomed to, the one that told her he thought his big sister was addled. Maybe she was. At the moment it didn't matter. She had a score to settle with the outlaws and she wanted to remind Decker of the promise he'd made.

They kept to the low places and angled toward the south. She was avoiding any trail the outlaws would have taken. It grew hot, but not as hot as the kitchen she'd worked in the day before. After a time she had them turn due west again. According to her reckoning this would put them on a parallel path with Culebra, separated by not more than several miles. Speed was essential. The outlaws would have stopped and made camp while waiting for her captor to complete his assignment. If she was right, she had a chance to get ahead of them. Then she would have to find Jake and Decker. She dared not let the outlaws catch them out on the desert alone, and she dared not think of failure. The next few hours, then the next few days, would determine their lives and their futures.

Chapter Thirteen

The man who called himself Culebra paced up and down, raising dust with every step he took. He was old for a man of thirty and he felt it. All the years of being on the run were taking their toll. But the early years had taken their toll, as well. A brutal, drunken father and a mother with too many children had given him nothing but misery. He'd left Ireland at the age of twelve. In the port city of Boston he'd improved his fighting skills out of necessity. From there he'd moved on to Philadelphia. When the Civil War broke out, he'd headed west to escape the conflict. It was somebody else's war, not his. The things they were fighting about meant nothing to him.

In the course of his travels he learned to shoot straight and to ride anything with four legs. It was after his arrival in Arizona Territory that he'd discarded his

Irish name. Lochlain Fitzgerald didn't seem to fit him anymore. It belonged to a bruised and hungry child, not the man that he'd become. He'd chosen Culebra the snake to replace it because snakes were dangerous, and he was dangerous. This was something that others began to learn.

The men who rode with him were useful but by no means were they his peers. McQuay was dull-witted with no imagination. Nettles had little in the way of backbone. The others were lacking in many ways.

However, it was Lockridge that was troubling Culebra the most. In spite of his best efforts, the man had managed to keep a step ahead of him all the way. He was certain that Lockridge, with the help of that kid they'd robbed, had brought gold from the mountains. It was the treasure that Nettles and McQuay had told him about. At first he'd thought it was just another windy story until they'd shown him proof. He pulled one of the strange gold coins from his pocket, taking pleasure at the sight of it. Plainly, it was old and unusual. Unquestionably, it was gold.

While they'd given him a few of the stolen coins in order to prove their story, he wondered how much the two had kept for themselves. He figured they'd hidden a portion before riding on to meet him. In their place, that's exactly what he would have done. But no matter. What lay somewhere ahead of him on those pack animals made a little stash of coins look puny by comparison. It appeared that Lockridge and his partner were intent on heading back to Arizona City. It was up to Culebra to see that they didn't get there.

After his enemies' surprise attack near the mountains, it had taken time for him and the others to regroup and resume the chase. Nettles had been wounded, while a near-miss had grazed his own thigh. Too late, they'd discovered the abandoned adobe shack. There was no doubt that Lockridge and four others had taken refuge there. The sign of this was everywhere, needing only to be read. Fresh blood stains told him that his enemies had sustained a hit as well. He hoped that the wounded man was Lockridge. Perhaps that would slow him down. Culebra and his men had pressed on in an attempt to catch up with them but they always managed to stay ahead.

McQuay approached him, hesitating before he spoke.

"Boss, how long do you plan on waitin' here for Kershaw to show up?"

Culebra scowled, for he was aware that he couldn't afford to wait much longer.

"We need those hostages. If he's not here soon, we'll backtrack a ways. If I end up losing all of that gold because of Kershaw's stupidity, I'll find him and break his bloomin' neck."

"While I was in Phoenix, I told him who to look for," said McQuay. "I got a real good look at the girl, and that kid who was with her must be her brother. Kershaw said that he'd seen 'em when they rode into town."

"Then Kershaw shouldn't have had any trouble finding them."

"What do you think their kinship is to Lockridge?" asked McQuay. "What I'm wondering is, will he be willing to trade the gold for their lives?"

This was a question that Culebra couldn't answer for sure, but his instincts told him that the two who'd been escorted to Phoenix were somehow important to his adversary.

"If that empty-headed Kershaw ever gets here, we'll find out," he replied.

McQuay backed off nervously. Culebra took satisfaction in seeing that the smaller man was afraid of him. It was a good idea to keep all of them a little bit afraid. Maybe they'd think twice about double-crossing him. Kershaw was as much afraid of him as any of the others and would have taken care to follow orders. He was beginning to worry that something had gone wrong to make him so late.

"Come on," he said at last. "Mount up. I can't waste any more time standing around here waiting."

They backtracked toward Phoenix until they came to the place where Kershaw had stopped with the prisoners. What Culebra read in the dirt confirmed his fears and made him furious. It was plain that three riders had stopped there. One had smoked a cigarette. That was Kershaw. Then two riders had taken off to the southwest, leading a riderless horse. Finally, there was a single set of boot prints that led toward town.

"Looks like he's had some trouble with the hostages," McQuay observed. "What do we do now?"

"Kershaw couldn't have gotten far on foot," said Culebra, his voice as cold as ice. "I'm going to find him and kill him, even if it costs me a fortune in gold."

None of the five men who were with him dared to speak out against what he was planning to do. They fell in behind him as he followed the boot tracks.

"We ought to be able to spot him before long," said Nettles who had taken to holding his wounded side.

The sooner the better, thought Culebra for he needed to get back on the trail. Unfortunately, that trail had split and he couldn't divide his men. He was going to have to make a choice between going after the hostages or following the gold. He couldn't afford to lose track of the gold and he needed the hostages to get it. Kershaw was going to pay for his blunder.

They came to a creosote bush from which a branch had been recently broken. From that point, an attempt had been made to wipe out the boot tracks. Kershaw was smart enough to know that they would be coming after him. The wind had risen and was blowing sand. This was helping to cover his trail as well. Still, Kershaw was most likely without water and Phoenix was the nearest source. A thirsty man would be headed for a drink.

It didn't take them long to find their quarry cowering in a depression of the landscape.

"Boss, I'm afraid I had some trouble," he said as he stood up.

There was a look of fear on his face and a deep purple bruise stained his forehead. Culebra aimed his .45 at the bruise.

"Kershaw, you're as useless as a four card flush," he accused.

Kershaw had been disarmed by the hostages. He had no defense. He was terrified. Culebra could scarcely contain his rage.

"I waited all morning for you to do a simple job," he said. "Now, thanks to you, a treasure in gold is getting farther and farther away from me. All you had to do was bring me a skinny girl and a half-grown kid, and you let them get away from you."

Kershaw started to plead for another chance when Culebra squeezed off a shot. While his partners watched, his lifeless body fell to the ground.

"Come on, let's get back on that trail and follow the hostages," Culebra commanded.

"But I thought you were going after the gold," said McQuay.

"That was my plan. But I've been thinking about it and, unless I miss my guess, the woman and the kid are on their way to find Lockridge. We'll simply find them and follow them to the gold."

They rode back to the place where the Sandovals had made good their escape. In spite of himself, Culebra had to admire their ingenuity in getting away from Kershaw. It looked like one of them had waited for the chance, and then knocked him senseless with a rock. But it shouldn't have happened. If Kershaw had been alert they wouldn't have gotten away. He figured the incompetent had gotten exactly what he deserved.

When they came to the banks Gila River, he gave the order to stop. The delay for water was a necessary one.

"Boss, what if they're holed up in those mountains, yonder?" asked Nettles. "We might never be able to find 'em."

"Then we'll just have to take the mountains apart. I want that gold. What's more, I want Lockridge dead. He's caused me way too much trouble."

They crossed the river and rode toward the mountains. But before they were able to get very far, the wind that had been rising all along became a howling fury. Culebra pulled his bandana over his face and lowered the brim of his hat as a shield against hurtling sand particles. The world was quickly obscured, as was the trail of the former hostages. But all wasn't lost for he had a hunch where they were headed. At least he knew the general direction.

He wondered just how much gold Lockridge and that kid had brought out of the Mazatzals. He knew from their tracks that they had three heavily loaded pack animals. If the loads were all gold, there was quite a lot of it. Quite a lot, indeed.

He had strength in numbers since Garcia and Hoskins had ridden out of Phoenix ahead of Kershaw. Hoskins had been with him the longest and was as capable as any who rode with him. Garcia was an excellent shot. That made five of them against Lock-ridge, his greenhorn partner, a woman, and a kid.

"Hey boss, this storm is gettin' real bad," said Hoskins. "Maybe we ought to stop until the wind lays."

Culebra hated to take anyone's advice. Advice was too close to an order. Without a word of reply he plowed on through the sandstorm. None of the others dared to drop back so they kept on going. The horses were nervous, though, and it was growing impossible for them to continue.

Minutes later, he had to give in. Making it appear that it was his own idea to stop, he reined up.

"Look for shelter!" he shouted above the howling wind.

They were trapped in a shrouded, other-worldly landscape, and finding shelter wasn't easy. When they did, it wasn't much. It was merely the leeward side of a low hill, but it afforded them a chance to rest and wait for calm.

"I don't reckon there'll be any sign of them hostages left by the time this is over," Hoskins said. "I'd hate to think we've lost 'em."

"We'll find them," Culebra assured him. "They're somewhere in those mountains and they're headed straight for Lockridge."

Culebra's instincts told him that he was right.

They waited out the sandstorm and left their sheltered spot just as the first stars were appearing. It was going to be a clear night.

"We've wasted far too much time," he told his men. "Let's ride."

There was enough night light so that Nettles was able to spot the campsite when they came to it.

"Over there," he said. "By those boulders."

The Sandovals had found a shelter of their own, which had protected them from the wind. Their tracks were still there.

"Let's go!" he ordered. "There's a fortune awaiting us and it's not far off."

Chapter Fourteen

Farley felt a sense of relief when he saw that he wasn't going to be pursued. Not that he'd expected Lockridge and that greenhorn kid to leave all of that gold behind and come chasing after him. On top of that he'd managed to be a big nuisance, and they had too much at stake with Culebra on their trail. He eased off so as not to tax the mare's strength and started thinking about the possibilities. In the beginning his intention was to find Culebra and resume his place in the gang, in spite of what his boss had done. But now he figured he'd be a fool to do that after Culebra had abandoned him to his enemies and caused the hardships he'd had to endure. Of course, he wanted satisfaction for Lockridge's part in his misery too. It was inhuman making him walk all those miles. But what he wanted most of all was to have the gold that was stuffed into those burlap bags—all of it.

Before he'd made good his escape, he'd managed to steal a pistol and a supply of ammunition. It was lucky for him that the Decker kid was easily distracted. If he'd been dealing with Lockridge, no doubt it would have been a different story.

He circled back until he came to a rise not far from where they'd made camp. He left the mare behind and crawled to the top. There he flattened himself against the ground so he could watch without being seen. The burlap sacks were piled below, bulging with their burden. The sight of them made his heart beat faster. The way he saw it, those sacks would compensate for all the painful miles he'd been forced to trudge in the desert heat.

Gold had the power to make a man dream and Farley did so. He pictured himself decked out in fancy new clothes, the kind that you bought in a big city store. He'd be wearing a tie and a gold stick-pin so folks would be sure to know that he was a man of means. Maybe he'd even have his picture took at one of them studios. What's more, he'd dine on the finest food and drink only the best liquor. Beautiful women would ask his name and seek out his company. He found himself smiling, and it was with great reluctance that he abandoned the pleasant daydream for reality. But he needed his wits about him, now. Since Lockridge and Decker hadn't pulled out, it meant they weren't likely to leave until they could do so under the cover of darkness. This would give Farley a chance to sleep for awhile, and sleep was something he badly needed. He stretched out on the ground, closed his eyes, and slept.

It was almost dark when he awakened with a start. His stomach was empty and growling its hunger. He had no food with him but he'd gotten away with a little of the water. He took a drink and did his best to ignore his stomach's complaints. Below, they were starting to break camp. He lay there watching as they rode off in the moonlight. Then he mounted the mare and began to follow, taking care that they didn't spot him. In his favor, they would assume that he'd high-tailed it out, never to return. They wouldn't be looking for him to come back alone for the treasure. They'd be looking for Culebra, though, and he'd be watching out for Culebra too.

They were covering the miles as quickly as the heavy laden animals could go. Farley was hard put to keep up with them. The thought crossed his mind about how unpredictable a man's life could be. He'd been Lockridge's prisoner a short time before. Now he was free and soon he'd be rich. What's more, he was going to make Lockridge pay—in more ways than one.

They were headed straight for the Gila Bend Mountains. He was sure of that because that's where he would be going if he were in Lockridge's place. If he could get ahead of them and pick them off, the treasure would be his for the taking. All he would have to worry about, then, was getting caught by his boss. But if he could kill Lockridge and his partner, it would be an easy thing to hide in the mountains near the trail and pick off his former partners, including the Snake himself.

Afterward, he would leave Arizona and go someplace else. California maybe, or Mexico. The mare he was riding was a fine horse and he would soon have others. For once in his life, things were going his way. If he could pull this off, he was going to be wealthy beyond his most outrageous dreams.

After a time he reined up. In the distance Lockridge and Decker were stopping beside the Gila River. From the shadows where he was hidden, he watched as they watered the horses and mules. Then they crossed over to the other side. He listened carefully for any sound of Culebra's approach and was relieved when all he heard was the desert wind. He waited, then, until Lockridge and the kid were well on their way before he moved from cover and headed for the river himself.

"Stinking desert," he complained to the mare. "It's either too hot or too cold."

He was ready for change. He was going to live a whole lot better than he'd ever lived before. But first, he had to keep his nerves steady and his eyes on the gold.

Chapter Fifteen

After he and Decker left the basin where they'd made camp, Jake took care to check his back trail from time to time. He knew that Culebra and his outfit wouldn't give up. Besides, Farley may have hooked up with the gang again. If so, he could lead them straight to the treasure. His caution paid off, for not long after they'd crossed the river he spotted a rider silhouetted in the moonlight. Whoever was trailing them was keeping his distance. The fact that it was a single rider puzzled him, though. It wouldn't be Culebra's gang and the rider wasn't an Apache either, for he didn't sit his horse like an Apache. Neither would an Apache have been so careless as to let himself be seen. That left Farley. The outlaw must have gotten gold fever and come after the treasure.

"We've got company," he said to Decker.

"How many?"

"Just one. It's Farley, most likely."

"Where is he?"

"Back there. He's staying well behind us, but he got a little careless and let me catch a glimpse of him."

"Strange," said Decker. "I had Farley pegged as the kind of fellow who'd run to his boss instead of doing anything on his own."

Jake had to agree.

"I expect that's true most of the time, but gold can draw a man like a magnet. Most likely Farley's had a chance to think about how all of that gold is better than a small share."

"Well, let him come along then, for I'd sure like to get my hands on that coyote. It'd be a pleasure to let him know how I feel about that clout on the head that he gave me."

Jake understood. He didn't much care for Farley either.

"We need to be in the mountains by daylight," he said. "It wouldn't do to be caught in the open."

What he didn't mention to Decker was his decision to hole up in those mountains instead of making a run for Arizona City. He didn't want to get caught on the open desert beyond, where they'd have no chance at all. It was still dark when they reached the foothills, giving Jake a sense of relief. They'd have a fighting chance now.

"You must have been through here before," Decker said.

"Once. Nate was here first, though, and he talked about his journey."

But even relying on Nate's directions and his own recollection, it wasn't easy to find his way. He had to grope for the narrow trail that he'd used before. It would take him deeper into the mountains where he would leave it and find a defensible position.

"I don't know what it is that you're up to, *amigo*," Decker said. "But I suspect that you have something in mind."

"I'm afraid you're going to find out since you'll be in the middle of it."

He grimaced.

"Now, why does that make me nervous? You know, Lockridge, I've learned an awful lot since I left Prescott. Riding with you has been an education."

In spite of the seriousness of their situation, Jake was amused when he imagined the very staid Judge Kemp considering his grandson's "education". By its nature, it was a far cry from reading law books in a back room. He said as much to Decker.

"You're right about that, and the lessons are harsher, but for the first time I've felt really alive. I don't think I was ever meant to be a lawyer."

Jake suspected that Decker was right. He couldn't imagine his partner clothed in fancy duds, trying to sweet-talk a jury with honey-coated words. Still, there was a lot of other jobs that he'd be good at. He'd just have to find one that suited him. That is, if they were able to get out of the mess they were in.

The narrow trail wound its way upward. It was dawn when they reached a vantage point that was shielded by several large rocks. Jake stopped. This natural fortress was off to the side of the trail and a little above it.

"Up there," he said, pointing. "That's where we'll stay. We'll be well-hidden, yet we can see anyone approaching for miles."

"Looks good to me," Decker approved.

They left the trail and climbed the steep slope. There, they tethered the horses and the pack mules. The boulders were large and situated so that they hid the animals as well.

"I think this is the next best thing to being in a fort," observed Decker as he looked around. "That entire gang would have to think twice before attacking us up here. And if they did, they'd be sorry."

It was fully daylight now. Jake pulled out the field glasses and took a look at their back trail. It was easy to spot Farley below them in the foothills. He'd kept on their trail throughout the night. Jake watched until the outlaw disappeared behind an obstruction.

He heard Decker come up beside him.

"Is it okay if I have a look?" he asked.

Jake handed the glasses over.

Decker put them to his eyes and turned in a wide arc.

"There's no sign of anyone else," he said.

"Don't fool yourself, Culebra is out there," Jake assured him. "I can feel it in my gut. He's just too smart to let us see him and there's places to hide."

"What do we do now?"

"We wait."

Throughout the morning that's what they did. But after mid-day, the wind whipped up a full blown sandstorm. Jake was thankful that the place he'd chosen was sheltered. Farley would be holed up someplace too.

"This storm ought to slow the outlaws down some," Decker said. "Out there on the flats, you wouldn't be able to see your hand in front of your face."

What he said was true. But the storm would abate. When it did, the outlaws would ride on. The lure of a treasure was too strong for them to quit. He was glad in a way, for he hadn't forgotten the score that he had to settle with McQuay. But for the time being, the storm raged on.

"This gets on a man's nerves after awhile," Decker complained. "I'm getting sick of the taste of sand in my mouth."

Jake understood what his friend was talking about for he could taste the gritty stuff too. The howling wind and the wind-whipped sand did, for sure, put a man's nerves on edge. It was like Nature was throwing a temper tantrum. But all temper tantrums end eventually, and this one would, too.

The elevation of the Gila Bend Mountains was lower than that of the Mazatzals. The vegetation was sparser, too. This meant there was less cover, but it would also make it harder for his enemies to conceal themselves.

Toward evening, the wind finally laid. It was a relief to them both. Decker removed his hat and shook the sand from its brim before putting it back on his head. Jake followed his lead, for his own hat had accumulated a thick coating. So had the rest of his clothing. He brushed himself off as best he could.

"Shouldn't Farley be showing up pretty soon?" asked Decker.

"Most likely. Stay alert."

They waited and watched for the outlaw but there was no sign of him.

"What do you make of it?" said Decker.

Jake didn't know.

"Maybe Farley found shelter and decided to spend the night or maybe he spotted us from below. If that's what happened, he may be sneaking around to get ahead of us. It could be that he plans to ambush us somewhere up ahead."

"Staying overlong in a shelter doesn't sound like something a man would do who's hot on the trail of gold. Maybe he's on the move like you say."

"We'll wait until dark and then we'll move on ourselves," he said, though he was reluctant to leave the safety of the boulders.

Soon after nightfall they readied the horses and mounted up. It seemed they were alone on the mountainside but he knew this wasn't true. His enemies were out there somewhere. They were simply unseen and that was when an enemy was the most dangerous.

In the bright moonlight, he could see a tall peak looming to his left. It wasn't as high as some others that he'd seen, but he guessed that it must be a few thousand feet from the desert floor. That peak would give him a sense of where he was, much like the North Star.

Thanks to the provisions that Decker had purchased in Phoenix, they were well-supplied with food. This was good because he couldn't use his gun to hunt. Gunfire would give their position away.

Soon after they'd made their way around a bend, Jake heard a rustling in the underbrush. It was off to the side and at least a dozen yards above the trail.

"Somebody's up there," he warned, drawing his pistol.

"Stop and put your hands in the air!" came an order. The voice was Miguel's.

"All right, my friend, haven't we been through this before?" asked Jake. "What in blazes are you doing in these mountains?"

"Jake!" cried Alicia. "We were afraid you were the outlaws."

They watched as the Sandovals rode down to join them. Jake was glad to be close to Alicia again, but fearful for her safety.

"What happened?" he asked.

"We were kidnapped by one of the outlaws," she said. "They were planning on bartering our lives for the gold, but we knocked our kidnapper in the head and rode away."

"Culebra was waiting for us," said Miguel. "I guess he must have waited a long time. We came a different way to the mountains as fast as we could to warn you."

"One of the outlaws knocked my brother unconscious," said Alicia. "He was tied on the back of a horse, and I was taken from my room at the cafe with a knife at my throat."

Jake didn't like having the image of this in his mind. He fought back rage.

"When I got a chance, I hit him with a rock and we took the horses," she went on.

"My sister is a lioness," said Miguel. "We remembered that you would be heading for these mountains so we rode as fast as we could. Culebra picked up more men in Phoenix."

Jake hadn't liked Miguel much at first, but it was turning out that the kid was all right.

"You must have gotten ahead of the Snake while he was waiting for your kidnapper to show up with you," he said.

"I expect so. Anyway, we were told that he and his men were waiting, and they probably wasted even more time backtracking to look for us when we didn't show up."

"Where's Farley?" Miguel asked.

"He escaped," said Decker. "And it was my fault."

"You're probably better off without him. You won't

have to listen to him whining and complaining all the time."

"Yeah, he sure is hard on a fellow's ears. The trouble is, we caught sight of him following us. Farley's after the gold for himself."

"We'd better get moving," said Jake. "We're lingering too long and wasting too much time."

Before they could go, a voice cut through the darkness.

"Now, ain't this a touching reunion."

It was Farley and he was holding a gun on them. He'd crossed the Sandovals' trail and followed them.

"I see you've come to return my horse," said Jake.

Farley laughed and the sound wasn't pleasant.

"Not likely. I've come to take charge of the rest of 'em, and the mules as well."

The light was dim and Jake managed to ease the dun away from the others. If he could draw the outlaw's fire, then Decker and Miguel would have a chance to take him.

"Throw down your weapons," Farley ordered. "You won't be needing them anymore."

It was time to act. Jake kicked the dun in the sides, drew the pistol that he'd recently holstered, and fired. Before Farley could get a shot off, the outlaw dropped his gun and fell from the mare.

"Stay put," Jake ordered, as he dismounted and went to look at the outlaw who was sprawled on the ground. He nudged him with the toe of his boot but there was no doubt that Farley was dead. Jake retrieved the pistol from where it had fallen and turned to the others.

"That's one outlaw that we won't have to worry about any more."

In the moonlight, he saw Alicia make the sign of the cross.

"I hope Culebra wasn't close enough to hear that shot," said Decker.

Jake hoped so too, but he wasn't betting on it.

"I reckon we'd better not stick around. The more distance we can put behind us the better."

They rode deeper into the mountains in single file. Jake was first. Then came Alicia, Miguel, and Decker. Jake brought along the mare that Farley had stolen. He was pleased to have her back. Miguel and Decker divided up the pack animals and the spare horse that Alicia had liberated from the kidnapper.

The terrain became rougher and the trail was more difficult to follow. This slowed them down at a time when they needed to cover the miles quickly.

As night was ending, he decided to leave the trail again. He was on the lookout for another sanctuary that would afford them a measure of protection. Sooner than he dared hope, he spotted one. At some time in the ancient past, a couple of boulders had tumbled from the top and had come to rest on the edge of the mountain.

"This looks like a good place to stop," he said.

Decker agreed.

"If they come looking for us, we'll have the advantage of position even though we're outnumbered."

He climbed down from the saddle and went to help Alicia. It felt good to put his arm around her slender waist. But her weight against his wounded shoulder caused him to wince in pain.

"Oh, I've hurt you," she said, backing away.

He looked into her large, dark eyes that were expressing her concern.

"I'm fine. I just have to favor my shoulder a little, that's all."

She reached out and took his hand, oblivious to the others.

"Will we get through this?" she asked.

He didn't know what to tell her.

"We're going to try," he said finally. "We're sure in blazes going to try."

Chapter Sixteen

Culebra stood looking down at Farley's body. He didn't know what to make of it. He had no doubt that Lockridge had killed him, but why had he chosen this time and place? It was plain that Farley hadn't been dead very long, so he was getting close to the treasure. According to the sign he was reading in the dirt, that boy and his sister had rejoined Lockridge and the greenhorn.

"Looks like Farley ran out of luck," said McQuay.

As far as Culebra was concerned he never was much account. But in death, he'd preformed a service. Culebra knew for certain, now, that he was on the right trail and the gold was only a short distance ahead.

Kershaw's carelessness had cost time and trouble, and he was starting to think that he'd lost his chance. This was just what he needed.

"With Farley gone, that makes one less that we have to split the gold with," Nettles observed.

Culebra had never intended to split with him anyway, not since he'd let himself be captured.

"Stop wasting time," he ordered. "Let's go find them."

He and the four men who still rode with him made their way to the trail. The tracks of the animals headed in the direction that he'd expected. Droppings on the ground were fresh.

"Keep a sharp look-out, all of you," he ordered. "You can't trust Lockridge to do the predictable."

He'd been doing some thinking on the matter, and it seemed to him that Lockridge was like a stray mutt that didn't look at all dangerous. But when you put your hand down to pet it, the cur would bare its teeth, jump on you, and tear your flesh. Lockridge also had more than his share of good luck. He'd had at least a dozen shares when he'd found that treasure and brought it safely down from an Apache stronghold. Lucky men could be dangerous, but luck had a way of running out.

Culebra counted his losses. Two men had died in the Apache attack on his way to the Mazatzals. Then he'd had to kill Kershaw. To top it off, Farley, who'd been captured, got his own self killed. He was left to make do with Hoskins, Garcia, Nettles, and McQuay. For the time being, he needed them. Still, he was loathe to divide the gold five ways. No doubt, there would be a showdown with Lockridge and his sidekick, as well as that kid and his sister. If any of his men got killed in that showdown, so much the better. But after he'd gotten rid of Lockridge and his outfit, he'd have no more need for a gang. It would be a simple matter to get rid of the survivors. They wouldn't be expecting a double-cross and he could kill them one at a time.

Experience had taught him that gangs were easy to build. Anyone with a grudge, greed, and a gun was a good candidate. If ever he wanted to form a gang again, the task would pose no problem.

He'd been thinking about how he'd spend the gold once it was in his possession. Those thoughts gave him pleasure. It was time for him to embark on a new life, one of ease and luxury. San Francisco would be the perfect city in which to launch it. With a fine mansion, servants, fashionable clothes, and easy living, he could take the rough edges off his manners. He'd also choose a fine name for himself, a presidential-sounding name, and no one would ever suspect that he was the bandit who'd called himself the Snake.

"Boss, I've lost their tracks," Hoskins announced, interrupting his daydream.

Culebra swore under his breath and rode forward to take a look for himself. The trail continued on through the mountains, but there was no sign of anyone having been on it for a long time. Lockridge and the others seemed to have disappeared, taking the gold with them.

"We've got to split up," he ordered. "They've taken to the side of the ridge. They're up there, somewhere."

"If they are, they could be hiding, waiting to pick us off," said Nettles.

"All the more reason to find them and get rid of them."

Culebra preferred to be on the offensive and he didn't like this turn of events. He sent Garcia, Hoskins, and McQuay on down the trail with a warning.

"Watch out for trouble, and don't stick too close together. Keep some distance between you. That way you're less likely to be ambushed and shot all at once."

It was plain by their faces that they didn't like what he'd told them to do. They knew better than to question his orders, though. Besides, the promise of wealth served to spur them on.

When they'd gone on their way, Culebra and Nettles took off from the trail and headed for the top of the ridge. The slope was steep for the horses, and they had to make their way carefully. But he figured that once they reached the top, he'd have a good overview. If Lockridge and his bunch were anywhere around, he'd be able to spot them. Meanwhile, the men that he'd sent down the trail would serve to divert the enemy's attention. At least he hoped so. Once he'd located his quarry, he could plan how to kill them.

Nettles was stretching to see as far as he could.

"There's no sign of 'em," he announced.

"Well, did you expect them to hoist a flag and wave it at you?"

"No," said Nettles, flustered by the rebuke. "But you'd think that with all of them animals they got, they couldn't just up and disappear."

"Well, there's lots of places around here to hide. Once we get to the top we'll be able to see a lot farther."

Culebra had grown sick and tired of sandstorms, heat, and hostile Apaches. He was also fed up with sleeping on the ground, enduring the cold nights, and eating whatever was at hand. He was more than ready to embark on the new life that he'd envisioned.

"Maybe they'll start shooting at Hoskins and the others when they see 'em riding down the trail," said Nettles. "If they do, we'll know where they are."

This was something Culebra had anticipated. If it happened, he'd be above them. It was a good position from which to launch a surprise attack.

Since caution had saved him many times, Culebra was cautious as he made his way upward toward the rocky spine. But there was no sign of his enemies.

Before they reached the summit, he ordered Nettles to dismount, and did so himself. There would be no skylining for Lockridge and the others to see.

"Have you got the spyglass with you?" he asked.

"Yeah, it's here someplace."

Nettles dug the tube out of one of his saddlebags and handed it over.

Culebra popped the telescoped sections out to their full-length and squinted through the lens.

"See anything, boss?"

"When I do, Nettles, you'll be the first to know."

Culebra brought the telescope to bear on each section of the land. In this way, he spotted the granite boulders. They were perched on a ledge about halfway up the side of the ridge, at a considerable distance to the west of where he stood. They were surrounded by mesquite and paloverde, which provided additional cover. Had he been Lockridge, he'd have chosen that very place as a hide-out. He moved the glass slightly and discovered what he was looking for. Among the paloverde several horses and a couple of mules were picketed.

"I've found them," he said, handing the spyglass back to Nettles. "They're sheltering in those boulders. I caught sight of their animals."

Nettles took his turn at the telescope, focusing it in the direction that Culebra had pointed out.

"It's them all right. We've got 'em now."

Culebra began making his plan. He would work his way over to a place directly above them without being seen. Then after the shooting started, he'd attack. They wouldn't know what hit them. He told Nettles what they were going to do.

"But how are we going to get over there without them spotting us? There's not enough cover betwixt here and there to hide our horses."

Culebra needed Nettles, at least for a little while longer, so he restrained himself and spoke calmly.

"We're going to leave them here. Grab your rifle and plenty of ammunition, and come with me."

Culebra carried his own rifle and ammunition as he led the way, keeping just below the crest of the ridge. He made sure to stay low, and to take advantage of what cover was present. This consisted mostly of olive-colored bursage, catclaw with its curved thorns, and creosote bushes. At one point, in order to stay hidden, they had to get down on their hands and knees and crawl. They were almost across the open space when he heard Nettles make a choking sound. Culebra glanced back to see what was wrong and spotted the serpent that he was named for—a sizeable rattlesnake. The reptile was coiled a few feet away from Nettles, and he could hear the rattles clearly. The snake had been sunning itself when Nettles surprised it. Now, it was ready to strike. Nettles was frozen, his face a picture of terror. The bad part of it was that the snake was close enough to strike Culebra, should its attention be diverted.

If Nettles had been the only one in danger, he would gladly have left him to his fate. But something had to be done and it had to be done quickly. He'd once watched a man die of snakebite, and it wasn't a pretty sight. Culebra tried to slow and calm his breathing. His heart pounded and his mouth was as dry as the desert wind. If he went for his pistol, the rattler would strike. His rifle, though, was in his hands. If he could squeeze off a shot quickly enough, he might kill the reptile before it injected its deadly venom. The shot would warn Lockridge, but he couldn't worry about that now. He could actually smell Nettles' fear, or maybe the fear was his own. With the ominous sound of rattles in his ear, Culebra eased his finger to the trigger. He thumbed back the hammer and moved the barrel ever so slightly to line it up with the rattle-snake's head. The move didn't go unnoticed. He squeezed the trigger and scrambled away as the shot reverberated and the snake's head disappeared.

Culebra sat back on his heels and trembled, both from the fear that had taken him over and anger at having been forced to warn his enemies.

Nettles crouched nearby, shaking and swearing.

"Shut up!" ordered Culebra.

It was like a slap and it shocked Nettles into silence.

"They know that we're up here now," Culebra said. "We've lost the advantage of surprise. Still, they're trapped and there's nothing they can do about it."

"What if they come up here and start shootin' at us?"

"Then we'll just have to shoot back."

"Where do you suppose Hoskins and the others are?'

He was wondering the same thing himself. By this time they ought to be engaging Lockridge and his rag-tag band in a gun battle. But so far, the only gun that had been fired was his own.

"I'll promise you this," he said. "If them three don't

do their jobs the way they're supposed to, I'm going to make 'em sorry they was ever born."

It was then he remembered that he'd already decided to do this, regardless.

Chapter Seventeen

Jake tried to make himself comfortable beneath the sparse shade of a paloverde, but every nerve in his body was taut. The outlaws were closing in. He could sense it. He glanced over at Alicia, who sat as if she were posing for a painting. Her colorful skirt was spread out around her, and her expression was serene. He wondered how she managed it. Unlike his sister, Miguel was pacing up and down with a worried look on his face. Decker was watching the trail. No doubt he was dreading the trouble that was almost certain to come riding down it.

"Hey, *amigo*," Decker called. "Maybe we ought to make a run for it instead of sitting around here waiting for something to happen. If we pull out of here right now, we might be able to stay ahead of 'em, maybe all the way to Arizona City."

"Maybe we can," said Jake. "But I sure don't intend to bet my life on it."

"But what if we're wrong? What if they gave up after Alicia and Miguel escaped and they're not following us at all? Except for Farley, who was alone, we haven't seen hide nor hair of any of them."

Jake noticed that the Sandovals were listening with interest. He needed to put a stop to Decker's notions.

"But what if we're right? Look, Decker, there's not much in this world that I trust, but two things that don't let me down are my knowledge of human nature and my instincts. Right now, both of them are telling me that the outlaws are on our trail and that they'll be here soon."

Decker thought about that for awhile.

"I think you're wrong," he said finally. "But you're the boss, so I'll go along with whatever you say."

"My brother and I agree," said Alicia. "There can only be one leader."

Jake was relieved that there would be no contest of wills.

Decker turned his attention back to the trail.

Jake knew that the waiting was getting on all of their nerves. He felt it as keenly as anyone. Still, he was convinced that this was their only chance to survive. He got to his feet and picked up his rifle.

"Stay put and keep alert," he ordered. "I'm going to take a little walk and see if I can catch sight of the outlaws. If they come down the trail, maybe I can worry them some before they get this far."

"Be careful, *por favor*," said Alicia. "Don't let them see you."

"I'll go with you," Decker offered.

"No. This is a one-man job, and you're needed here."

Jake left the kid with a doubtful, disappointed look on his face. But everything he'd said was true. This was a job for stealth, not numbers.

He made his way carefully along the lower part of the ridge, taking care to hide himself in case anyone was on the trail. The sun was high, warming the land a little beyond comfort. He hadn't been long on his mission before he heard the sound of a rifle somewhere above him. Without thinking, he ducked. This was something he hadn't expected. He'd been looking for an attack from below. He was also surprised that he wasn't the target. He squinted into the sun, trying to catch a glimpse of the shooter.

Then, as if the shot had been a signal, three of the outlaws suddenly appeared. They headed down the trail in the direction of the boulders where his friends were waiting. The gang had split up so they could attack from two sides. He had little time in which to act. Decker and the Sandovals would have to hold off the three, while he went after the ones on the ridge. He was thankful for the warning shot, but he wondered why it was fired. Certainly not as a signal, as he'd first thought, for it had destroyed their chance of surprise.

He worked his way upward toward where the shot had been fired. His rifle was slung on his back, and he kept low to take advantage of the sparse cover. He thought it was strange there was no sign of their horses. His hands and knees were taking a beating, for at times he had to crawl. Then, with no further warning, war broke out below with a barrage of gunfire. It was then he caught sight of the two outlaws. They were rushing to attack his friends from above. He recognized one of them as Nettles. The other was Culebra.

While Jake watched, Nettles took aim at the boulders where Decker and the Sandovals were holding out against the other gang members. Jake grabbed the .45 at his hip and squeezed off a shot. Nettles fell. Culebra saw him and fired. The bullet found its mark and Jake was thrown off balance by the impact. He found himself sliding and rolling down the slope. Near the bottom, he ended up in a catclaw. Its thorns caught hold of his shirt, and the shrub-like tree provided him with cover. Culebra, believing he'd been killed, had turned his attention to the others.

As Jake rescued his shirt from the thorns, he saw that it was bloody from the bullet wound. With one quick movement, he ripped a strip from the bottom. Then he used it to tie his bandana in place, stanching the flow of blood from his side.

In the distance, gunfire was still being exchanged. He needed to get back into the action. He managed to get to his feet, but before he was able to get very far, the shooting stopped as suddenly as it had started. Jake feared the worst.

He started to run across the rugged ground and fell. The impact sent a shock of pain ripping through his body. Then he lost consciousness. When he opened his eyes, he heard nothing. Two buzzards were circling above him, considering whether he might provide sustenance. He tried to move and felt a sharp pain from the new wound. *The outlaws are trying to make a sieve of me*, he thought wryly. *No, they're trying to make me a dead man and they failed—twice.*

He lay still a moment, willing himself to overcome the dizziness and the nausea. He'd already lost a lot of blood, and now he was losing even more. With supreme effort, he managed to get to his knees.

He had to find out what had happened to his friends. He feared the worst. Finally he managed to stand and he shook his head to clear it. Then he moved on. He kept low and advanced from cover to cover, for the outlaws might still be there.

When he got closer to the boulders, he was able to look down and see what was going on. Alicia, Miguel, and Decker were all bound hand and foot. Culebra had rejoined his men. One of them had a gray beard and he favored his right leg when he walked. One of them was dark with a handle-bar mustache, and beside him was a fellow whose face reminded Jake of a weasel. Either the graybeard or the weasel had to be McQuay.

Jake lay flat on the ground with his rifle ready. He waited, for he dared not make a move with his friends trussed up the way they were.

"Alas, it is all over for you," he heard Culebra say

to the prisoners. "Your friend, Lockridge is dead and you are helpless."

"I don't believe you," said Alicia. "Jake is still alive."

Culebra smiled, something he must have been unaccustomed to doing.

"I had the privilege of killing him myself," he bragged. "Now, I'm going to leave the three of you tied up here, while we relieve you of your horses and pack mules. You may survive for a little while, but without water, you won't survive for long."

"Wasn't that what you said the last time you robbed me and left me to die in the desert?" Decker asked.

Culebra walked over and kicked him hard. Decker moaned in pain.

"I'd kill you now, but it would be too easy," said the outlaw. "You're going to die slowly and you're going to get a chance to think about your fate. So will your companions."

While Jake watched, the outlaws took the horses and mules, the supplies, and the gold. Then, without a backward glance, they headed down the trail. He waited until they were out of sight and earshot before he made his way down to the prisoners.

"Lockridge, you're alive!" Decker exclaimed, looking like he'd seen a ghost.

"They told us that you were dead," said Alicia. "But I knew they were lying. If that had happened, I would have sensed it."

Quickly, Jake released them from their bonds. Miguel noticed his wound.

"It looks like they shot you, *amigo*. I think that you're one tough *hombre* to kill."

"Let me look at that wound," Alicia ordered.

Jake was glad to lie down for a minute. Much as he wanted to go after the outlaws, he couldn't since they'd taken the horses. In fact, they'd taken everything. Nate had been wrong about a man being able to make a chance for himself. Sometimes there was nothing left to make a chance out of. Sometimes a man had no choice but to give up.

Chapter Eighteen

"We've got to do something," Decker said as he rubbed the circulation back into his extremities. "After all the trouble that we've gone through to get that gold, we can't let them steal it."

"Besides that, we have to find water soon," said Miguel.

"I'm afraid it's all over," said Alicia. "We've done our best, but there's simply nothing more that we can do."

Jake struggled to remember something that was nagging at him. In his weakened state, he wasn't thinking clearly. But there was something about Culebra and Nettles that he needed to remember. Then it came to him. They'd never have gone to the effort of climbing that high ridge on foot when they could easily have ridden. Yet, when he saw them, they were sneaking down the slope to ambush Decker and the Sandovals on foot. There could only be one answer. They'd left their mounts somewhere up on the ridge. After they'd stolen the gold and fresh horses, there wasn't time or the need to retrieve the mounts they'd left behind.

He struggled to his feet.

"I think I know where we can get a couple of horses," he announced.

The others looked at him in surprise.

"Where?" Miguel wanted to know.

Jake told them what he'd surmised.

"You're far too weak to go after those animals on foot, Jake," Alicia scolded. "Let Miguel and Decker go."

He had to agree.

"Go up toward the top of the ridge and head east," he instructed. "I'm willing to bet that you'll find them hobbled up there someplace."

"If they're up there, we'll find 'em," promised Decker.

Jake watched them leave and hoped that he was right. He'd taken one of the canteens with him when he'd gone to scout the trail, which meant that they had a little water. With two horses and a canteen, they might be able to survive.

"Do you think we still have a chance?" Alicia asked.

"There's always a chance."

"The numbers are even now," she said. "It's four against four."

This was true, but everything else was in the outlaws' favor. They had the horses and the weapons. They had the gold and a big head start.

Jake and Alicia didn't have to wait long before Miguel and Decker came riding down the slope. He'd been right about the abandoned horses.

"Now, we need weapons," said Decker as he dismounted from the big *gruello* that Jake had spotted Culebra riding more than once.

"We have the Spencer and my .45," he said. "It's not much to go up against them with, but it's better than nothing."

"If it'll help, I have the gun that I took from our kidnapper," said Alicia. "When the outlaws captured us, I hid it in my skirt."

Jake felt uncommonly pleased. Another pistol would make a big difference. He handed the Spencer rifle to Decker, keeping the .45 on his hip. Since Alicia opted to keep the gun that she'd confiscated, Miguel was left weaponless. It was plain that he didn't like it much, but there was no help for it. They were lucky to have any weapons at all.

"We'll have to ride double and take it easy on the horses," he said. "It's in our favor that they don't expect to be followed. That way, they're more apt to take their time. As far as they're concerned, we're all buzzard bait."

"We have very little water," said Alicia. "Especially when you have to divide it among the four of us."

Jake shared her concern, but he had an ace in the hole, one that Nate Lockridge had dealt him.

"I have the good fortune to be related to the man who knew every watering hole between the Mazatzal Mountains and Arizona City," he assured them. "He imparted that knowledge to me, so we'll find water. If it's any comfort, we'll also be crossing the Gila River again. It winds around so it flows on the other side of these mountains."

"Thank goodness," said Alicia. "And bless the man who informed you."

They mounted up. The Sandovals shared the handsome sorrel, which would have brought a nice price in town, while Jake and Decker took the big *gruello*.

The gang had gotten a head start, but Jake planned to close the gap. The outlaws were sticking to the trail and their tracks were easy to follow. When, at last, the ridge above them gave way to an overlook, Jake had them stop. Luckily, he'd taken the field glasses with him, so they hadn't been confiscated by the outlaws.

"Wait here, I'm going to have a look," he said.

While they waited, he crawled out to the edge. There, he scanned the area before him. In the distance, he spotted Culebra and two others on horseback. The trail had taken them lower on the mountain as it took them farther away. It puzzled him that there were only three outlaws when there should have been four. He wondered what had happened to the fourth man.

Maybe he'd doubled back for some reason. Perhaps Culebra had changed his mind and wasn't satisfied with leaving the prisoners to die of thirst. Maybe he'd sent a man back to shoot them. Whatever the reason, one outlaw wasn't accounted for. This was a dangerous unknown.

He stuffed the glasses back into the pouch and crawled away from the ledge.

"See anything?" Decker asked.

"Yeah. There's three of 'em down there. But one man is missing."

"Should we start worrying?"

"He's a wildcard. Who knows what he's up to. But we need to watch out for him."

Jake was able to remount with only a little help. The blood around his wound had clotted and he was confident that the bullet had passed through. Ordinarily, he'd have Decker or one of the others pour whiskey into it to clean it, but they had none. The niceties would just have to wait.

The *gruello* started off down the trail at what seemed like a plodding pace.

"Are we ever going to be able to catch up with them?" Decker asked.

"They don't know that we're after 'em. Since they're not running from anyone, no doubt they'll stop and make camp somewhere."

"And that's when we catch up."

"You've got a keen mind, Decker."

"Just wanted to know what you had planned," he said mildly, ignoring the jab.

It was late evening when Jake ordered them to stop. His side was throbbing, and it was hard to keep his mind off the pain. Seeing that he was hurting, Decker offered to help him down.

"Thanks," he said. "Now, will you get the field glasses for me."

Decker fished them out of a saddlebag and started to hand them to him.

"Unless I miss my guess, they should be making camp about now," said Jake. "Decker, why don't you work your way over to the edge and see if you can spot where they are. Just don't let them see you."

His partner looked pleased to be given the responsibility. He left them and was back within a few minutes to give his report.

"They're down there all right. So is the gold. They have the horses and mules picketed and they're making camp."

Jake felt a sense of jubilation. Now was their chance.

"How many men did you count?" he asked as an afterthought.

"Only three, *amigo*. That fourth man hasn't turned up yet."

"That's very peculiar," said Alicia who'd been listening. "If they'd sent him back, it looks like we'd have run into him by this time."

Jake had to agree. It was peculiar.

"Here, Miguel, you're going to need this," said Alicia, handing over the pistol she'd been carrying.

"Gracias," he said.

"Let's be on our way," said Jake. "And from here on out, try not to make any noise."

They continued on the trail as it wound downward toward the outlaws' camp. The sun was below the western horizon, and a gentle breeze stirred the foliage on the mountainside. It was a far cry from the raging wind that had whipped up a sandstorm the day before. Alicia draped a blanket around her shoulders like a shawl for the air was beginning to cool. Before long, they could smell the smoke from the outlaws' campfire. When they were close enough to see the flames, Jake signaled them to halt.

They dismounted quietly. Alicia, who had no weapon, held the horses. Decker clutched the Spencer carbine, and Jake and Miguel drew their pistols. Compared to the enemy, they were poorly armed. Still, if they could manage to surprise the outlaws, it would even things up a little.

Leaving Alicia behind, they spread out as they approached the camp. Jake saw Culebra, Mustache, and Weasel sitting around the campfire. Graybeard was the one that was missing, but Jake had a hunch that Weasel was McQuay. The three of them were eating, drinking coffee, and trying to out-brag one another. They were sitting close to the firelight and making a lot of noise, and these were things that prudent men would never do. They thought they had nothing to fear and they'd let their guard down.

Jake avoided looking directly into the flames for they blinded a man's night vision. He figured that Decker and Miguel were both savvy enough to do the same. They all crept closer to the camp while the outlaws remained unaware of their presence.

While he waited for his partners to get in place, Jake watched Culebra take the coffeepot and start refilling his cup. The outlaw must have sensed that he was being watched, for when he finished he looked up and saw Jake. Without an instant's hesitation Culebra dropped the cup, flung the pot, and went for his gun. Jake fired the first shot. Then he hit the dirt and rolled to the side.

When they saw Culebra go for his gun, McQuay and Mustache scrambled away from the campfire. They crouched in the shadows and fired in Jake's direction. One bullet came so close that he could feel the breeze from it. He had little in the way of cover. Only some scrub stood between him and the three outlaws who were trying to kill him. Then Decker and Miguel joined the battle. This wasn't to Culebra's liking.

"Forget the others, Garcia! Shoot Lockridge!" he yelled. "He's hiding over there in that brush!"

Before Garcia, who was Mustache, could follow his boss' order, he was felled by a shot from Decker's carbine. Jake aimed for Culebra. The Snake jumped aside. The head outlaw and McQuay were the only ones left now. While Jake was trying to locate Mc-Quay, he and Culebra made a break for the brush, firing as they went. To Jake's dismay, they were headed straight to where Alicia was waiting. He had to head them off.

Culebra spotted Alicia standing there holding the horses. With a sweep of his arm, he knocked her aside and climbed on the *gruello*. McQuay, who was right behind him, took the sorrel. Ignoring his wounds, Jake sprinted toward the horses but he was too late. Culebra leaned down and grabbed Alicia, dragging her into the saddle with him. Then he took off at a gallop.

Decker and Miguel came running up.

"They have Alicia," he said. "We've got to go after them."

They ran back to where the outlaw had picketed the horses. Jake threw a saddle across the dun's back and tightened the cinch. The others saddled up too. The gold was stacked nearby, but no one gave it a thought.

The outlaws had headed back the way they'd come. It was fully dark, now, but there was enough moonlight to see by. They were regaining the altitude they'd lost as they'd descended to Culebra's camp. The horses that the outlaws were riding had been ridden double for a long way. The ones Jake and his partners were on were fresh. He was trusting this to make a difference. They were entering a particularly dark stretch when he heard a woman scream. Alicia was trying to warn them. A shot was fired and Jake reined up. He and the others threw themselves from their mounts and drew their weapons.

"All right Lockridge," came Culebra's voice. "Throw down your guns or the girl dies."

"I thought your plan was to trade her for the gold," he said.

"You don't have the gold and I'm going back to get it."

"What about the fourth member of your outfit who's been missing for awhile? What's to stop him from going back and taking the gold for himself?"

"With a little help from me, he stepped off a cliff. That's what should have happened to all of you. Then you wouldn't be causing me trouble."

Jake turned and whispered to Miguel.

"Keep him talking," he said. "Beg for your sister's life—anything. I'm going to try to get around behind them."

"I'll go too," said Decker.

"No. Stay here. If they make a run back for the gold, it'll be up to you to stop them."

"You're running out of time!" yelled Culebra.

"Please don't hurt my sister," pleaded Miguel.

Jake was well on his way. He kept to the shadows as he circled around behind where the outlaws were holed up. Miguel was keeping them distracted as he stalled for time.

"There ain't nothin' to discuss," yelled McQuay. "Shut your trap and throw out your guns."

Jake could see them now, just below. Culebra was

holding Alicia close and his hand was covering her mouth. One jump and he'd be beside them.

"You've just run out of time!" shouted Culebra. "I'm going to kill the girl."

"No!" screamed Miguel. "If you do you'll have nothing to bargain with and I will kill you with my bare hands."

Jake leaped and landed against the outlaw, shoving him to the ground. He slung Alicia aside. McQuay turned to aim his pistol but Jake dove for his legs, knocking him backward.

"Come help!" cried Alicia to her brother.

Jake was on top of McQuay, driving punches into his body. Culebra was cursing and Alicia was screaming. He heard the others coming.

"I'll take him," said Decker as he grabbed McQuay and dragged the disarmed outlaw to his feet.

Jake turned to Culebra. Alicia was scratching and hitting the Snake, preventing him from grabbing his gun and shooting them. Miguel appeared and started to help, but Culebra's hand found his pistol. He got to his feet in a crouch.

"I'll kill you, Lockridge!" he yelled.

He brought up his gun, but Jake was close now. He reached out and knocked it aside. The gun went off. Jake grabbed his wrist and twisted. Miguel got him around the neck from behind and squeezed. Culebra went limp and dropped the weapon.

"You're not going to believe this," said Decker.

Jake turned to see what he was talking about. His

partner was holding McQuay in his arms. The outlaw had a hole in his shirt and blood was leaking from the hole. The bullet that Culebra had intended to kill him with had killed McQuay.

"I guess Culebra saved the folks at Arizona City the cost of a jury trial and a hangman," said Decker.

He was right. Nate's murderer was dead and Nate was avenged. Jake only wished he'd been the one who'd killed him. But in a way he figured he was, since he'd slapped the gun away as it was being fired.

"What are you going to do with me?" asked Culebra. "I'll make a deal with you. You can have all the gold if you let me go."

Jake laughed in his face.

"The gold was mine in the first place. It's mine now. And you're in no position to bargain. I guess somebody's going to have to hire a hangman after all."

He tied the outlaw's wrists securely and hoisted him onto the back of the *gruello*. All the while Decker was keeping him covered. Then they mounted up and headed back toward the camp and the treasure. He thought of how close he'd come to losing Alicia and involuntarily shuddered. He wanted to keep her with him. He knew that now for certain.

Back at the camp, Alicia found some whiskey in one of the outlaw's saddlebags.

"Come let me clean and dress your wound," she said. "It's long past time this should be done."

He gave in and let her care for him. It was a pleasure to have her close and feel the touch of her hands.

Culebra was bound and under the watchful eye of Decker.

"You won't get me to town," said the outlaw. "You're fools to even try."

"What do you want us to do?" asked Miguel. "Do you want us to shoot you? For what you've done to my sister, I would gladly oblige."

It sounded to Jake like the outlaw was blustering. He figured they ought to take turns watching him throughout the rest of the night. Come morning, when they were rested and the horses were rested, they would journey on.

He felt weak and tired but before sleeping there was something he wanted to tell the others.

"I've changed my mind about the way I'm sharing the gold," he said.

"What!" said Decker. "You can't do that. You promised."

Jake struggled to sit up.

"Wait and hear me out," he said. "I'm dividing it into thirds. A third for you, a third for me, and a third for Alicia and Miguel."

He heard her gasp.

"Is this true?" she asked.

"Yes. You see, I've always wanted to marry a woman of means, and since you and your brother are sharing a third of the fortune, I'll be doing just that."

The next thing he knew, she had her arms around him, kissing him. Decker let out a war whoop of joy that echoed across the mountain valley. Miguel, alone, had the good sense to watch the prisoner.

Jake felt light-headed by the time she'd finished kissing him. She took hold of his hand.

"Thank you, *mi querido*. Sharing in the treasure makes up for having to leave those gold coins in that mattress in Phoenix."

"They'll have to stay for someone else to find, for I doubt if we'll be going back that way."

"And where will we go?"

"Where do you want to go?"

"Somewhere that's pretty and peaceful."

"Wherever that is, we'll start tomorrow."

On the seventh day of their journey from the outlaws' camp, they arrived at the town where he'd started. They delivered Culebra to the jail, and banked the gold. Then Jake went alone to his uncle's grave.

"I got 'em all, Nate," he said. "Me and my friends did, anyway. I got the gold, too, and there's something else. I found the woman that I'm going to marry."

He stood there in silence, trying to imagine how Nate would reply. He knew he'd be pleased.

Back at the hotel, he met the others.

"What are you going to do now, Decker?" he asked.

"I think I'm going to start me a newspaper. Maybe right here in this town. I think my grandfather wouldn't be too disappointed at having an editor for a grandson."

"Are you going to send word to him?"

"Yes, though I doubt if he'll believe what's happened to me."

Decker had changed so much for the better that he doubted if the Judge would even recognize his grandson. He turned to Alicia.

"Would you like to stay here for a while until we decide where we want to go and what we want to do?"

"Yes. I think this would be wise and Miguel has agreed."

Jake went out then and bought himself a new suit. Next, he went to the bathhouse for a bath. The water was warm and the smell of the lye soap cleared his head. Miguel and Decker came along before he was finished.

"My sister is getting fixed up for her wedding," said Miguel. "There's a church at the other end of town and the priest is willing to marry you this afternoon."

"I've got a few things to do," Jake said. "But I intend to be there. I trust you fellows will be there too."

"Of course," said Miguel. "I am to give the bride away."

Jake dried off and got dressed in his new suit. Then he went to the barber shop and got his hair cut and his beard trimmed. Back at the hotel lobby, he saw Alicia coming down the stairs. She'd done some cleaning up and shopping of her own. The sight of her took his breath away. She was wearing a soft green dress and a white lace *mantilla.*

"You look beautiful," he said.

She simply smiled and took his hand.

"Your brother tells me that a priest is waiting for us."

"That's right," said Miguel as he and Decker entered the hotel wearing new suits. "Shall we go?"

Jake offered his arm to his bride and they walked together to the church.